Time Warriors: Part Two

Written by Tom Tancin

Cowritten by Chris Wolf

This series is dedicated to the many people that helped us over the years. There are so many that it is impossible to list them on this dedication page. Although this book may have been written by two people, many more were involved in the process. They know who they are, because we made sure of it.

-To Ann, you mean more to us and this series than you realize. I wish there was a way to show you that. Thank you for your support, it is greatly appreciated.

Part One
The Experiment
The Secret of Atlantis
The Master of Time

Part Two(**)
The Armies of The Zodiac
The Return to Paradise
The Elements

Part Three
Ancient Egypt
Discovery
Realization

Part Four
Quest
Destination
Forces of Time

From the Author

Here you are, about to read part two of the series. I thank you for your interest. I hope you really enjoyed part one and I hope you really enjoy the rest of the series. In this book, and the next two after this, you will find the addition of a section that recaps the books prior to the current one you are holding. That way, you can recall what happened in the series prior to what you are about to read. And just like in the first book, this one and the others to follow, will have a preview of what is coming next in the series.

Now, on to what I have to say about what you are about to read. These missions were written when Chris and I were in the prime of high school. I believe that this is the most creative book of the series as it throws out, to the reader, some interesting and spectacular ideas about the time periods the characters visit.

In this book, you will join the warriors in a battle against twelve extraterrestrial armies. The Armies of the Zodiac is Chris' favorite mission. I enjoy the addition of the characters in the zodiac mission. William, Steph, and Amanda will each be important in the series as it continues. The fifth mission takes the reader back to 'paradise' to revisit the nightmare of the first mission. However, this time a whole new twist is thrown in. Mission six is one of my favorites, second only to mission nine (in part three). I think the way Heather's character develops in mission six allows her to show that she is extremely important to the team, and to me. Also, the creation of Karma's character in mission six was my idea and I grew to love the character.

A piece of advice for reading this book, take notice to the friendships between the various members of the team and how they begin to change. This book is the foundation for what is going to come in part three, and it is crucial to realize how it all starts. Each character begins to change, and the overall change for the series will be significant. A lot of the decisions and judgments that characters make in this book will come back to haunt them later. But as always, enjoy the book for what it is, a science-fiction work. I thoroughly enjoyed writing this book and I hope you get a sense of that as you read it.

Sincerely,

Tom Tancin

Recap of the Series

The United States government created a time machine and needed to test it. A quest to recruit graduating seniors from around the country began. Each state had competitions, with the winning team going on to nationals. Fifty teams, one from each state, competed against each other in Washington D.C. for the chance to be the first humans to set foot in time. The competition came down to Team Pennsylvania and Team Missouri. Team Pennsylvania, consisting of our heroes, won the competition. Team Missouri became the backup, rescue team for any emergencies that could arise.

Team Pennsylvania made up of TJ, Heather, Chris, and Krissy, took the first trip into time. When TJ forgot to put the time period in, the machine started to act up. Chris accidentally hit the emergency warp button and got the team in a world of trouble. The time machine blew a circuit in the time records and left the team stranded in time. Their environment was a prehistoric paradise ruled by giant reptiles. Team Missouri was rounded up to begin a rescue operation. However, they had other plans. Danny, the leader of Team Missouri, and his dad were the ones who caused Team Pennsylvania to get stranded in the prehistoric paradise. Danny and his team were set on killing their competition and becoming the prestigious Time Warriors.

However, our heroes put up a fight and ended up returning home safely. Team Pennsylvania became the Time Warriors and were asked to move to Washington. Time travel was open to the public and the team had the responsibility to regulate it. The government discovered that four criminals were set on stealing the secret of Atlantis. However, they had no idea what the secret was. The Time Warriors followed the criminals to Atlantis. Once there, the team met a native boy who knew more about the island than anyone. They soon discovered that the boy was the banished son of Poseidon. His name was Triton, and he held many powers and secrets. Following the clues left by the criminals, Triton and the Time Warriors found themselves at the door of Poseidon's temple.

Inside, they discovered that the criminals were looking to steal the Codes of Atlantis. The codes held the key to the island's civilization. They were written by Poseidon himself. The Time Warriors battled with the criminals, but were unsuccessful in stopping the criminals from escaping with the codes. Once the codes left the temple, the island began to sink, taking everyone with it. The criminals did not make it off the island alive but the Time Warriors were saved by Triton.

Once they returned, the team quickly disintegrated. Krissy was unhappy with the stress and risk of the team and so she resigned. Chris requested a less chaotic schedule so he could be with his new girlfriend, Kelly. Meanwhile, TJ and Heather learned that there was a group trying to take over the world using time travel. The group was based out of Missouri. A coincidence? Probably not. The leader of the group, Tyler

Brooks, was calling himself the Master of Time. He had unimaginable knowledge about time travel and how to control it. Tyler kidnapped Heather and led TJ on a wild-goose chase through time. TJ was able to save Heather, but Tyler had another plan. Plan B was to kidnap the president's son and lead TJ and Heather on a chase through time.

TJ and Heather pleaded for Krissy and Chris to help, but they were blind. Krissy was letting her fear stop her from saving the world. Chris was allowing his girlfriend to stop him. However, he soon discovered that Kelly was Tyler's sister. Chris left Kelly and recruited Krissy to help. Tyler knew that in order to defeat the Time Warriors he would have to keep them separated. Once united, the warriors were unstoppable. Kelly and her associate Nick kept Chris and Krissy distracted, while TJ and Heather battled with Tyler. Tyler unleashed the KATS, animals that thrive to kill, to take care of the warriors. Once, Chris and Krissy realized that they were just being distracted, they made it their goal to reunite with TJ and Heather. They were successful and soon battled with Tyler and his associates as a team. The warriors defeated Tyler after a tough battle. After the battle, the warriors made a pact to stand united. They were either all in or all out. And TJ, decided to unite with Heather in marriage. TJ and Heather were married in a ceremony between Time Warriors: Part One and Time Warriors: Part Two.

Seven Months Later… The Legacy Continues

Mission Four:

The Armies of the Zodiac

CHAPTER ONE

We all sat around a campfire in the woods. It was Chris, Krissy, Heather, and I. We were camping with a family of three avid campers. We had decided to take this vacation because we needed a break. It was a cold night. The kind of night that was typical for the end of November. However, the cold weather never stopped the family we were with and we wanted relaxation. The father was in his forties and he had been camping all his life. His family told us that Scott was really good at telling campfire stories. His wife was sitting next to him, her name was Joann. Joann was also in her forties and had a love for the outdoors. We knew their son Bryan because he was carrying out his internship at the Department of Time Travel. He was looking to get involved in the government and they sent him to our building. He just started a few weeks prior to the camping trip.

"Ok, I will start the first story," Scott said. Heather moved over toward me and laid her head on my shoulder. Scott added some wood to the fire and it got warmer. "Around 3,000 B.C. in England, the people started to have a severe interest in the sky. People have always been amazed by the sky but this was different. This was fear. They became aware of the threat that the unknown was posing to them. They had been told all their lives that when the sun, moon, and stars lined up in a certain path that something horrible would be unleashed. This had been passed down for generations. From what we know about their culture, they were passing it down for over five thousand years. Anyway, they found a map of the sky and how it would look when this evil would plague them. They decided to create the map on the ground out of rocks." Bryan cut in laughing.

"This is so fake. Like they actually did this," Bryan was mocking his dad. We all looked at him.

"This is true," Scott said, "I believe it with my heart. I would bet my life on it."

"Let your father continue," Joann added as she gave Bryan an evil look.

"I think it's interesting," Heather said.

"Alright," Scott said, "I'll go on. Anyway, they built this map out of rocks that they got from a location miles away from where they built Stonehenge. They carried the heavy rocks that weighed thousands of pounds uphill and down. They used all of their knowledge about levers and propped the heavy stones up with logs. They used months of planning mathematically to accurately depict this map. They knew that if they made this map line up exactly how the story said it should, they would know well in advance when this evil would be unleashed. It took them a few years to build this structure, but not as long as the research says. Most research says that it took them thousands of years, when in fact it only took them three or four years. When they finished they stood in awe."

"So what is the evil," Bryan said sarcastically, "did the rocks come to life?" He started to laugh.

"No, it is much worse than that," Scott answered. Just then we heard howling from the woods. I looked and saw blue eyes glowing in the dark. Actually there was quite a few of them. I stood up and grabbed a stick. The wolves walked down to us. One jumped at Bryan. He pushed it away. Scott ran over and helped him fight it off. One went after Krissy and she screamed as it snapped at her leg. Chris went over and kicked it in the nose. Heather backed up right into one. I ran over and kicked it in the head. Just then I heard Bryan scream. We looked to see two wolves attacking his leg. Scott tried to get to Bryan but was stopped when three wolves cut him off.

"Joann," Scott yelled, "get in the car." Joann ran toward the car but was taken down by the wolves. I grabbed a stick and ran to the fire. I lit the stick on fire and started swinging it at the wolves. One jumped on Heather and knocked her down but I hit him with the stick and lit him on fire. The wolf howled in pain and ran into the woods. I helped Heather up. Chris and Krissy ran to the car and went inside. Heather and I ran over to the car and hopped in.

"Where's Bryan and them," Heather said with concern. I looked around in all directions but could not see them.

"Let's go back to the city," Chris told me. "We can send a rescue team when we get back." I nodded my head and started the car up.

When we got back to Washington we contacted the forest rangers and sent them to the woods. We stayed home the next few days because we had scheduled off. Scott, Joann, and Bryan were found alive but were not in good shape. They were taken to a hospital and put in intensive care. As far as I know, they each had multiple surgeries to repair their injuries. But we never saw them again.

CHAPTER TWO

Meanwhile there was a team of scientist studying Stonehenge in England. The lead scientist, Amanda Smith, was extremely interested in the purpose of Stonehenge. She wanted to know why the ancient people felt the need to build such a marvelous structure. She believed that it was built for a reason similar to what Scott believed. Amanda was a very good scientist, one of the best in England. Her son, William, was walking around the structure with nothing to do. William was seventeen and was always helping Amanda with various projects. Amanda did not study Stonehenge for a career, it was her hobby. She worked in a lab studying and creating various chemicals that were requested by organizations. She not only worked at, but was one of the managers of one of the most secure labs in the world. Amanda was in her forties and devoted to her job.

Amanda was born and raised in the United States. Her grandparents lived in England and so she would visit a lot. She fell in love with England. In her late teens, while visiting her grandparents, she met a young English soldier. They fell in love and got married. She moved to

England to live and work. Her husband left the military and began working at the lab. Amanda got pregnant with William and took a leave of absence from work. Her husband was killed in a lab accident while she was on leave. To help cope with the death, Amanda began researching various things on the side. She would take William with her. Now, she was on to Stonehenge. However, William was a teenager and wanted nothing to do with researching with his mother.

Amanda picked up the brush and started to brush the dirt from the altar stone. It was in the center of the structure and to Amanda it was the key to the mystery. It was layered with dirt and very weathered.

"Did you find anything mom," William asked.

"No, nothing that makes sense," she answered. "If only I could find the missing link. But I think it has something to do with the zodiac."

"What do you mean the zodiac?"

"That's the force," she answered. "That's the evil."

"So you are saying that the same things that tell our future and represent us are evil," he summarized.

"Yes," she answered as she scurried around trying to find more clues. William broke out laughing. He almost fell over that's how hard he was laughing. "You are only seventeen," his mom said. "You have a lot to learn. You have no right to laugh at your mother."

"Wait," he said as he continued laughing so hard he couldn't speak, "you are the one telling me that the zodiacs are the evil force and yet I am the one that has to learn a lot." He continued to laugh as he walked away. "The zodiacs, evil." He was still chuckling. Amanda just shook her head in disgust.

"I'll show that boy," she said, "just like the rest of the world, they'll stop laughing."

Meanwhile in Washington D.C., I was doing some research on my computer. I was determined to find out more about Scott's theory. I never thought about why Stonehenge was built, but now I was extremely curious. I pulled some graph paper from my desk drawer. Then I grabbed a ruler, compass, and protractor. I started to draw the map as it was shown on my computer screen. Someone knocked on my door and then Heather stuck her head in. I hurried to put the drawing in my desk. She smiled.

"Are you still trying figure that story out," she said with a giggle. I just gave her an angry look. "Sorry," she said, "I didn't realize it meant that much to you."

"Aquarians are dedicated to their work," I said.

"Ok, Mr. Aquarian," she said, "can you stop for lunch?" Once again I gave her the look.

"Not really, I think I got something."

"Alright," she said, "I'm going with the others to get some lunch." She came over and gave me a kiss and I gave her some money. She walked out and closed the door. I got the map out and started again.

Heather went into Chris' office. "He's not going, he's still trying to figure that story out," she told Chris. They walked out into the hall and met Krissy. The made their way to the first floor and out of the building. It was extremely cold and snowing like crazy. The city employees were decorating for Christmas. Chris led them into a sandwich shop and they ordered their meals. They sat down at the table and started to eat. There was a TV with the news on.

"Now to our top story," the newscaster said as he shifted through the papers in front of him. "Right now, the prime minister of Britain is meeting with our president about global security issues. Yes that is correct, England found a clue that shows a threat to the world. That's all we know."

"I wonder what that is about," Heather said.

"Somehow, I have a feeling this involves us," Chris said.

"Of course, we always get the global security problems," Krissy said. "As if they can't give it to the FBI or the CIA."

CHAPTER THREE

When they came back to the office Heather came in and looked at me. I looked up from my work.

"I wish you would just take a break," she said. "We haven't spent anytime alone and we are married." She walked over and locked the door. She came over and sat on my desk. She took the map and pushed it to the side. Then she kissed me. I just looked at the ceiling. "What's wrong," she asked.

"Nothing why," I answered.

"You won't even kiss me and I'm your wife."

"I am just too busy."

"Well, I am sorry for holding up your work if that's more important than me." She hopped off my desk and slammed the map down in front of me. She stormed to the door, unlocked it, and opened it. Then she looked back at me and shook her head. She walked out and slammed the door.

"Heather, I-I," I said but I just stopped. It was pointless to argue with her, you can't win. When I had the map finished I just stared at it. Chris walked in and he looked at me.

"Are you stupid," he asked.

"Don't start," I told him.

"Do you know you are going to lose her," he asked.

"No, we're married, remember?"

"Not for long," he continued, "she is in her office crying. Now I suggest if you want to spend the rest of your life with her you listen to me."

"Alright, what do you suggest?"

"Stop your work for one night and spend time with her." He walked out.

"YEAH, THANKS CHRIS," I yelled, "BUT I ALREADY KNEW THAT!!!!" I took my hand and pushed my hair back and then slammed my head on my desk.

That night Chris drug us all to a dance club. When we walked in the strobe lights made me dizzy. The music was so loud I couldn't hear myself think. I was too interested in cracking the story to be at a dance club. Chris led Krissy to the bar to let Heather and I alone. Heather led me to the dance floor and started to dance. I just stood there watching her. She grabbed my arms and started to shake them. Heather didn't like to dance or go to clubs but she would do anything to get me to pay attention to her. Finally she realized that shaking my arms wasn't going to work so she started dancing crazy and trying to make me laugh. I started to smile. Chris saw her trying and went over to the DJ and made a request. This song continued and she ended up getting even crazier. I started to laugh. Then she grabbed my arms again and started to swing them. I pulled away and went over to a nearby table. She just shook her head and danced over to Chris. She pulled him out to the dance floor and started to dance with him. He was dancing too. Krissy came over and sat down at the table. When they realized that wasn't working, Chris went up to a guy sitting at a table by himself and led him to the floor to dance with Heather. Heather started to dance with him and Chris came over and sat down. He smiled at me. I frowned at him and kept an eye on Heather. She knew this was making me jealous and so she danced even more.

After that song was over the DJ played a slow song and Heather slow danced with that guy. I looked at Chris in shock.

"You didn't," I said in anger. "Tell me you didn't."

"I did," he replied as he smiled. I punched the table. I got up and walked out of the club. Heather ran out of the club after me. Chris and Krissy followed her. I hopped in my car and drove off. Heather was screaming the whole time.

"Great plan," Heather said to Chris. "I thought you said that would work. Shows you know your friend."

"Hey," he said, "he's your husband. I think you should know him better. Come on, I'll take you home." They hopped in the car. Chris dropped Krissy off at her house. He dropped Heather off at our house and drove away. She walked up to the front door but it was locked. She started to pound on the door. I was ignoring her. She kept pounding on the door.

"TJ," she screamed, "open this door now!!! Right now!!! Come on it's cold!" She kept pounding. I walked over and opened the door. She came in and slapped me in the face. "Don't ever do that again," she said.

"Well," I replied, "I can't believe you did that to me."

"It was Chris' idea."

"So, since when do you listen to Chris?"

"Since you spend absolutely no time with me. TJ you are always working. I am your wife, I want to spend time with you too."

"But this is how I am. I need to finish this."

"You will, but can we please just have the rest of this night to relax? We're newly weds and we didn't even have a honeymoon."

"Ok, I said." She went over and put on a CD. She came over and sat down next to me on the couch. She laid her head on my shoulder and we fell asleep.

CHAPTER FOUR

I woke up when I heard someone talking. I looked up and saw Krissy and Chris walking around. I looked at Heather and she was still sleeping with her head on my chest. I scooted up and put her head on a pillow. Then I walked into the kitchen and poured a glass of water. I sat down at the table and took a drink. Chris and Krissy came into the kitchen and sat down. Chris threw a newspaper at me. I looked at the front page and read the headline.

U.S. AND BRITAIN DECIDE TO MEET WITH UNITED NATIONS ON GLOBAL THREAT. THEY MAY LOOK TO THE UNITED STATES TIME WARRIORS.
The President of the United States and the Prime Minister of Britain decided that for the safety of the world they need to go to the United Nations. The threat may have happened in the past so they are going to decide whether or not to send the Time Warriors. This breaking news comes from an all night discussion by the two leaders and was just announced early this morning. When questioned, the two leaders said it has something to do with Stonehenge and outer space.

I stopped reading and couldn't believe it. More like I didn't want to believe it. I threw it back at Chris. "Looks like we may have a new mission very shortly," I said. "Big surprise."

"We said we would continue," Chris added. I got up and walked back to the living room. Heather was getting up.

"Good morning," I said as I sat down next to her.

"Morning," she replied and then kissed me.

"I think we are going to have a new mission," I told her.

"Really," Heather said. "What is it?"

"Go into the kitchen and read the newspaper." Heather got up and walked into the kitchen. Chris handed her the newspaper and she sat down at the table. She read the paper and then handed it back to Chris. She got up and got the water jug out of the refrigerator.

"Nothing to say," Chris asked.

"Yeah, Chris," Heather said sarcastically as she poured herself a glass of water. "Actually I have a lot to say, I'm just holding it in."

"Really," he said. "I couldn't tell."

"Chris, don't start," Heather said. " You know I don't like to be bothered in the morning."

"You don't like to be bothered at all," Chris mumbled.

"What," she snapped.

"Nothing," Chris replied.

"I'm going to get ready for work," I told them. I walked upstairs and took a shower. Then Heather got her shower. At ten o'clock we left for the office. When we got to the office there was a ton of information sitting on our desks. I sat down and started to page through the information. It was on Stonehenge and the time periods it was built in. The phone rang and I picked it up.

"Time Warriors, TJ speaking," I said.

"TJ, this is the President," the voice answered.

"Hello, Mr. President," I continued. "What can I do for you?"

"I am going to meet with the United Nations today to discuss the next step. I was wondering if your team would consider working with the rest of the world, not just our country?"

"I suppose we could."

"Ok, I will meet with the UN and let you know what we decide." I hung up the phone and walked over to Heather's office. She was playing solitaire on her computer.

"How would you like to be part of a global team," I asked her.

"No thank you," she said. "Right?"

"Actually," I continued, "I told the President we would."

"Oh, well thanks for consulting with us."

"Well I had to answer him. He is meeting with the UN today."

"I think he would've understood that you have to ask your team. We are a team right?"

"Yes, but I ha…"

"But nothing," she yelled. "We are a team. Consult with us first."

"What would you have done? Would you tell the president that he has to wait to meet with the UN," I screamed. "I'm sorry Mr. President but I have to talk to my team first. They are the center of the world you know." I walked out of the office and slammed the door. I walked to my office and slammed my door shut. I picked up the pen holder and threw it across the room. The pens flew everywhere. I took the stack of papers and threw it all over the room. I pushed the chairs over and kicked my desk. Suddenly a great idea came to me. I ran out of my office and down the steps to the lobby.

"I'm going out for a little while," I told the secretary. I walked outside the building and signaled for a taxi. "Take me to the airport," I ordered the driver. When I got to the airport I walked up to the ticket booth.

"Can I buy four tickets to London," I asked.

"When would you like to go," she asked.

"As soon as possible," I replied.

"I have a flight from here to London on December 5th, is that ok?"

"That's fine," I said, "only four days, that's fine." She gave me the tickets and I showed her my badge so she put it on the government's account. I walked back to the parking lot and got another taxi back to the offices. I made my way upstairs to my office and cleaned up the mess I made. When I was finished, I sat down at my desk. Heather and Chris came in.

"We're going to a dance club again tonight," Chris said.

"Not me," I said. "I won't. Not after what happened last night."

"But I want to spend time with you," Heather said.

"Then we go somewhere else," I replied, "but not to a dance club."

"We can go to a Washington Redskin football game," Chris said.

"Whatever," I said. "But we're going to England in four days."

"I don't want to go to a football game," Heather said. "Why are we going to England?" I thought about how to answer that. I knew if I said to research the story she wouldn't go.

"I planned it to spend time with you in romantic London," I answered. "Like the honeymoon we never had."

"Oh, that's so sweet," she said and she walked out. Chris followed her out and I smiled.

CHAPTER FIVE

The President stood up. "Ladies and Gentlemen of the United Nations," he started, "earlier this week we got word of a threat to the world. It involved Stonehenge and why it was built. The only way to find out what threat we are dealing with, is to send my team back in time to when Stonehenge was built and have them investigate. In order to do this we need to all agree that they can work on behalf of the entire world." The President sat down and Britain's Prime Minister stood up.

"I agree with the President," he said. "They saved us from the Master of Time and I am confident they can handle this. We'll send them back to find out what threat we are facing and how soon it is going to plague us." The leader of Germany stood up.

"Ja," he said, "we have a problem and we need to fix it. But if we make it a global team I think there should be some members from other countries." The head of the UN stood up.

"We need to vote," he said, "first who thinks the mission is a good idea?" Everyone raised their hands. "How many want to allow the Time Warriors to work for the world when needed?" Everyone raised their hands. "Then it is decided."

Meanwhile we were sitting in the conference room, just talking. "We need to take time to ourselves," Krissy said. "We are working way too hard and we don't even have a mission yet."

"I agree," Heather said. "We should wait until we have a mission before we start taking all this action."

"I still want to know what we are doing tonight," Chris asked.

"How about we go to dinner and then a play," Heather said.

"Yeah," Chris said, "that sounds relaxing."

"I don't like plays," Krissy said, "but at least I can sleep." They all looked at me.

"What," I asked, "I am waiting for a call from the President."

"So wear your beeper," Heather informed me.

"Alright," I agreed. "I can't win anyway."

"I'll go make the reservations and get the tickets," Krissy said.

"I'll help you," Chris said. They walked out of the conference room. Heather went over and turned on the radio. I got up and walked out of the room. I started walking up the steps towards my office and Heather followed. She ran as fast as she could up the steps to catch me.

"TJ," she said, "wait." I continued to walk up the stairwell and she followed. When we got to our floor I went into my office. I grabbed my cup and went back down the steps to get coffee. She followed me down again. I made my way to the coffee pot and filled my cup up. Dr. Johnson ran over in a hurry.

"Get out of the building," he said trying to catch his breath. "There is a bomb threat from a follower of the Master of Time."

"What," Heather cried in fear as she looked at me. "We have to get out of here. Let's go."

"I have to get the information," I said. I ran down the hall toward the stairs.

"No," Heather screamed, "forget the information!" I didn't listen and kept running so she followed. Dr. Johnson ran out of the building because he didn't know what to do. I was running as fast I could up the steps and I didn't know Heather was following me. Just then I heard the explosion and the steps started to crumble. I fell down and hit my knee on the step. I stood up and continued to run up the steps skipping the steps that were falling. Heather fell with the rumble and the steps under her fell. She grabbed on to the steps that were left and was hanging there. There was another explosion and the ceiling started to fall in.

"Help," Heather screamed. I looked down and saw her hanging there. I ran down and pulled her up. Then I continued up the steps and she followed.

"No," I said, "get out of the building."

"I won't, if you won't," she responded. There was another

explosion and more of the ceiling fell. There was a fire at the top of the steps and the water sprayers were on. The water was pouring down the steps making them very slippery. I made it to the third floor and opened the door to the hall. The entire place was destroyed. There was smoke everywhere and pieces of the ceiling blocking the hall. I jumped over some of the huge pieces of concrete. I ran into my office and grabbed the folder of information and the map. Heather was waiting in the hall and I met her. We ran to the stairs again and looked down.

"We won't make it down," I said. "There are too many gaps."

"Take the elevator," she said.

"Not in this situation," I answered.

"What else are we going to do?"

"True." We went back into the hallway and ran down to the elevator. We got in and I pushed the button for the ground floor. There was another explosion and the elevator stopped and tilted sideways. Heather fell and hit her head on the wall. I went to her and held her head, examining it. The elevator tried to move again but it was jammed in the angle it was in. It was bouncing and we were holding onto the wall.

"What do we do now," Heather asked.

"We try to get out of the elevator," I answered,. "I'll boost you up if you open the trap door." I picked her up and she punched out the trap door. Then I boosted her out of the elevator.

"Oh my god," she said, "Floor one is below us and we can't get past the elevator." I hooked my feet into the bar on the wall and hopped up. I grabbed onto the edge of the elevator's top and pulled myself out.

"We have to climb up to floor two and then go down the steps," I said. We climbed up the ladder on the side of the wall. I forced the second floor door open and we ran down the hallway. When I got to the stairwell, I opened the door. I was going to step out but realized there were no steps. "We have to get around the elevator," I said. We ran back to the elevator shaft and climbed down the ladder. I stood on the elevator, thinking about how to get around it. "Jump on it," I said. "Loosen it so it will fall." We jumped up and down. It slid a little but wouldn't go any further.

"Alright," I said, "you continue to jump on it. I'm going inside and I'm going to run into the left side to try and get it back on track. When I do it is going to fall so grab onto the cable and hang there. I will quickly hop out of the elevator and grab the cable.

I hopped into the elevator and started running into the left side with my shoulder. It hurt but I had to try to get it back on track. "Hurry," Heather said, "the smoke is building up." I heard her coughing. I continued to run into the side of the elevator.

Meanwhile outside, Krissy and Chris returned and they saw a lot of smoke coming from the building. They looked around for us but couldn't see us. "Where are they," Chris asked Dr. Johnson.

"Inside," he answered. Krissy and Chris ran in. The elevator was almost back in the track. Heather was still jumping but she was coughing like crazy.

"I can't breath," she said. She fell over. I heard her hit the elevator with a thud. The elevator started to fall. I jumped up and pulled myself out of the elevator. The elevator was speeding up. I grabbed Heather by the arm with one arm and the cable with the other. I held the cable tight and Heather's arm even tighter. Heather started to wake up. She looked down and screamed.

"You have to climb up," I told her. She climbed up my legs and over my head and held on. Then I grabbed the cable with both hands. The elevator crashed in the basement and the dust and smoke rose quickly.

"Take a deep breath," I said, "then we'll climb down as quickly as possible." We took a few breaths and then a deep one. We started climbing down quickly. Chris and Krissy heard the elevator crash and so they opened the door at the first floor. They looked up and saw us climbing down. Heather slipped and fell. I grabbed her foot as she passed me. She swung over to the cable and grabbed on. She was hanging on, upside down

"Let go," she said. I let go of her foot and she turned herself around. We continued to climb down. When we got down to the first floor door we had to jump from the cable to the door but it wasn't going to be that easy. Heather started swinging and when she felt she had enough momentum she let go and flew over to the door. Krissy and Chris caught her arms and pulled her up. Then I did the same and we ran out of the building. We stood outside the building as the firefighters sprayed the building with water.

"You went up for information," Heather said, "and you didn't even bring it."

"Yes I did," I said as I pulled it out of my shirt.

CHAPTER SIX

I woke up on December 5th and looked over to see Heather still sleeping. The phone rang but I ignored it. I got out of bed and packed my clothes. I loaded the car while Heather was in the shower. Finally we were ready to leave. We drove to the airport and met Chris and Krissy. We got on the plane and flew to England. "So what do you have planned," Heather asked, "I hope it's romantic."

"Yeah, it is," I said, "it's really romantic."

"I can't wait," she said. I knew that she was going to kill me when she found out that we were going to England to work on a mission.

When we landed in England a group of British scientists were waiting for us. A woman scientist walked up to us. "Welcome to England," she said. "I'm Amanda Smith. This is my son William." Krissy looked at William and seemed pleased.

"My name is TJ, and this is my wife Heather. That's my best friend Chris, and my cousin Krissy," I said.

"Well, then I suppose we should be on our way," Amanda said. "I got you rental cars." Amanda led us out of the airport. We got in the cars. Krissy rode with Chris, William rode with Amanda, and Heather rode with me. I followed Amanda and Chris followed me.

"Where are we going," Heather asked me.

"Stonehenge," I answered.

"Wait," she said, "I thought you said this was a romantic vacation."

"Things changed," I responded, "the President asked us to come here."

"You didn't tell us."

"I know. I felt you wouldn't come if you knew it was work."

"You're right. I wouldn't have." I continued to follow Amanda. When we got to Stonehenge I got out of the car. Heather chose to stay in the car with her arms crossed in anger. Chris and Krissy walked up to Heather and she explained why she was mad. I walked around looking at the structure.

"Over here," Amanda said. I walked over to her. "I learned for years that the zodiac was the evil force that caused the ancient people to build Stonehenge. I have book upon book at home about the legend. I just don't know if it is true."

"That's where our team comes in," I said. "We're going to head into the past tomorrow."

"Well," Amanda said, "if you leave tomorrow then you should get something to eat and get some rest. Why don't you come back to my house?"

"Alright," I answered. Heather didn't talk to me at all during the ride. When we got to her house I stepped out of the car. I looked at her house, it was huge, and pretty expensive. It was a brick house with a balcony sticking out from the upstairs. She led us into the house. When we first walked in there was a chandelier. I looked around and saw a huge entertainment center. Heather looked at me in surprise.

"These scientist must make a lot of money," Krissy said. We followed Amanda into the dining room which had a marble table. The hutch was made of glass.

"William," Amanda said, "take our guests into the kitchen for something to drink." William signaled us to follow him into the kitchen. There was an island in the middle. The floor was linoleum but she had rugs around. William grabbed four sodas from the refrigerator and threw them at us. The phone rang and William answered it. After a few minutes, he hung up the phone and made his way into the dining room.

"Mom," he said, "Steph is on her way over. She wants to meet the Americans."

"Ok," Amanda said. "What do you want for dinner?"

"Americans like Pizza," William said. Krissy walked in and smiled at him. He smiled back. "I'll show you your rooms," William continued, "follow me." We followed him up the marble steps with the gold railings. They twisted as they went up. When we got upstairs he led us into the first room. "This is my room." I looked around. He had a stereo system with surround sound. He had a huge bed and big glass windows. He had a walk in closet on the side and a huge television with a DVD player. He led us out of his room and past the next room. "That's my mom's room," he said. He led us down the hall. He walked into the next room. "This is for Krissy." It was very similar to his room. Then we walked down and the next room he stopped at was for Chris. Then finally he took Heather and I into ours. Ours was also very similar to his. He went downstairs as we settled in.

Steph walked in and he greeted her. "The Americans are upstairs," he told her, "they'll be down for dinner, it's pizza."

"Of course," Steph replied, "they're Americans." She walked into the dining room and sat down. Steph was skinny and average height. She had blonde hair down to her shoulders and she was very well kept. She had blue eyes. She was very beautiful. She was William's best friend but nothing more. Upstairs, Heather and I were laying on the bed. Chris came in.

"Are you ready to go down," he asked.

"Yeah," I replied as I stood up. Heather got up and we walked downstairs and into the dining room. At the first glimpse of Steph, Chris stopped. Steph stood up and looked at William.

"Nice," she said.

"What," William asked. She pointed over at Chris and I.

"Check her out," Chris said.

"Wow," I replied. Heather looked at me. "I mean ouch, don't hit me Chris."

"I didn't," he answered. I elbowed him and he shut up. He realized that Heather was there. "I'll talk to you later," he continued. Heather looked at him with the evil eye. "I mean, never," he corrected himself. We sat down and Amanda brought out the Pizzas.

"So," Steph said, "are you two together?" She pointed to Heather and I. Heather shook her head yes.

"They're leaving to go back in time tomorrow," William said.

"William, you should go with and take pictures for me," Amanda replied. He looked at her and agreed.

"I want to go too," Steph said. Chris looked at me. Heather gave me the evil eye as if to say don't even think about it.

" It's your decision, Chris," I said to save myself from Heather.

"Ok, you can go," Chris jumped quickly to say. Heather looked at Chris then at me.

"Excuse me," she said, "I want to go lay down." She got up and went upstairs.

"You two need to talk," Chris said. "You need to work these problems out. Go ahead, we'll talk later."

CHAPTER SEVEN

I got up from the table and walked upstairs. I walked down the hall to our room.

When I went in Heather was crying on the bed. I walked over and sat down by her. I touched her hair.

"Leave me alone," she said.

"Heather we need to talk," I said.

"No we don't."

"I want to work our problems out. The only way to do that is to communicate. Look, what is the problem if we add two new members? Or before that, tell me what is wrong."

"You want to know. This could take awhile." She got up from the bed and started pacing back and forth. "Well, let's start with you working too much. TJ, we are married now, we need to spend more time together. Next, you need to cut the jealousy crap. That thing at the dance club, was just to get you to dance. Another, start treating us like a team, we are a team. Finally, treat me like your wife, you don't even kiss me half the time."

"Alright, I'll try to listen to those suggestions. But what about the new members."

"William is fine, he can stay, but Steph has to go."

"Wait, didn't you just tell me to cut the jealousy crap, now you have to."

"I'm am not jealous of Steph."

"Yes you are."

"No I'm not!" She stormed out of the room and slammed the door. Chris was coming down the hall. She pushed by him but he grabbed her arm and drug her back to our room. "Let go," she screamed at Chris. He pushed her in our room.

"Now, I am locking this door and you are not coming out until you resolve this," he said. He took the key that was in the door and locked it. He walked away. I sat down in the chair and Heather laid down on the bed. We didn't talk for about ten minutes. Finally I decided to try and work it out.

"Heather, I'm sorry," I said. "I want you to know that I have no interest in Steph."

"I'm sorry too," she replied, "I have been rather moody. TJ all I want is to spend some time with you. And I want you to make a promise."

"Anything," I said.

"Promise me that we'll start a family and we'll stop the missions for some time."

"I promise." I walked over and sat down. I kissed her. "I love you," I said. "And I want to start a family. When the time is right, we'll walk away from the team and make our family the priority."

Meanwhile downstairs, Krissy and William were talking. Steph was sitting on the couch. Chris came down and sat down next to Steph and she smiled at him. William put a movie in and they watched it. After the movie, Chris realized that we were still up in the room. He ran up the steps and unlocked the door and walked in. We were both sleeping on the bed. He closed the door and smiled.

The next morning Chris woke up and went downstairs. He met Amanda in the kitchen and she was making breakfast. "Good morning," Chris said.

"Morning," Amanda replied. "How did you sleep?"

"Good, thanks."

"Are you ready for the big trip?"

"Big! This is little compared to the last time."

"That bad, huh?"

"You wouldn't believe. So how long have you been working on this case?" Just then William and Steph walked in.

"Hey mom," William said.

"Morning Amanda," Steph said, *"and Chris"* Chris just rolled his eyes.

"Where did you sleep last night, Steph," Amanda asked.

"With William," she answered.

"What," Amanda continued in shock.

"On the floor," William replied. "Relax mom, we have nothing more than a friendship."

"That makes a couple of us more fortunate now doesn't it," Chris said.

"What do you mean," Steph asked.

"Nothing, just an inside joke," Chris answered. "I have to go get Krissy, she needs to get up and get ready. After all it takes her at least four hours to make herself just ugly." William just shook his head. Chris went upstairs and knocked on Krissy's door. "Hey Rip," Chris yelled, "wake up." He didn't hear anything. He went in. "Hey ugly, wake up."

"I thought you were already up," Krissy replied.

"Yeah, I was up a while ago, they asked for the more scary," he answered. She picked up her shoe and threw it at Chris. She missed Chris by a mile and hit William who was passing by the door.

"Sorry," Krissy said. Chris walked out of her room and William went in.

"I got to get the lovebirds up," Chris said as he walked toward our room. He knocked on our door. "Get up, lovebirds."

"We are up," we answered. He opened the door and came in.

"So did you work out your problems," he asked. He was surprised that we were showered and ready to go. Heather was standing in front of the mirror combing her hair. It was still wet.

"Yeah," I answered. I walked over and hugged Heather around her waist and kissed her on the cheek.

"How," Chris asked. "Oh wait, never mind, I don't want to know." He walked out of the room and downstairs. On the way past Krissy's room Chris saw Krissy and William sitting on the bed. "That is not good," Chris thought to himself. He hurried past. He walked to the stairs but didn't see the mop that Amanda was using to clean the floor. He tripped and fell down the whole flight of marble stairs. "Son of a... that's gonna leave a mark." Steph came running over.

"Are you alright," she asked.

"Am I bleeding," Chris asked.

"If you were, I wouldn't be standing here," she answered.

"That's good to know," Chris replied. Just then he saw Krissy walking to the top of the steps.

"Krissy," he yelled in pain. "Watch out for the..." Before he could finish she tripped and came tumbling down the steps. Chris tried to move but was too hurt and she landed right on top of him. Chris let out a cry, "...mop!"

"Are you ok," William yelled from the top of the steps.

"Krissy," Chris said.

"Yes," she answered.

"Did you ever have anything that weighs three times the amount of you laying on your chest?"

"No, I can't say I have."

"Well I do, now get off!" Krissy rolled off. Chris laid there and took a few deep breaths before getting up very slowly.

"So whose hungry," Amanda asked. Chris looked at her.

"I am," Krissy said.

"You are always hungry," Chris replied.

"So?"

"Take a break, come up for air."

"Shut up," Krissy said as she walked into the kitchen, "pig."

"Pig," Chris said, "at least I ain't the brother of Shamoo." Steph laughed.

"Ain't ain't a word," Krissy replied as she walked to the kitchen. "And it ain't in the dictionary and you ain't gonna use it anymore."

"That would be my saying," Heather said as her and I made our way down the steps. Chris, Steph, and William walked into the Kitchen.

"Well," Chris said, "record breaking time to find the trough I see."

"Shut up," Krissy commented with a mouth full of food.

"Any left for us," Chris asked. "Or did you eat it all already?" Krissy took another big bite and looked at Chris.

"As I said before," she continued with so much food in her mouth that you couldn't understand her, "shut up." Heather and I walked in.

"Are you guys ready," I asked.

"I'm not done eating yet," Krissy answered.

"Too bad," Chris said, "you ate enough already. Your weight will collapse the warp zone." She turned and looked at Chris.

"Let's go," I said, "but let's drop the attitudes before we do." Krissy got up from the table and we walked outside the house. "William and Steph are going to have to hang on to one of us," I continued. "We don't have enough belts."

"Steph you can go with T…" Chris said. Before he could finish Heather punched him in the gut. "Me," he blurted out with a gasp for air. Steph smiled at Chris. William grabbed on to Krissy's arm. Steph jumped on Chris' back.

"Hang on tight," Chris said to Steph. "Don't let go."

"Don't worry," Steph replied, "I don't intend on ever leaving go."

"Oh great," Chris muttered under his breath.

"Let's go," I said, "on three."

"Good luck," Amanda said.

"Ready," I said. Heather looked at me with a look of anxiety and fear. "One, two…"

"Wait, wait," Krissy said.

"Now what," Chris complained.

"On three," Krissy asked, "or after three?"

"One," I continued, "two, three." We pushed the buttons on our belts and warped through the warp zone.

CHAPTER EIGHT

We appeared at what seemed to be festivities of the ancient people. There were bands playing music and people dancing. Then they saw us.

"There's more of them," they yelled. They picked up swords made out of rock and started to run toward us.

"Wait, wait, wait," Chris screamed. "More what?" They came running at us.

"More running," I said, "go!" We all started to run except Krissy.

"Maybe they have some food," Krissy said. "All that traveling mades me hungry."

"If you don't run," Heather said, "you will be their food." Krissy started to run. They cornered us against a wall.

"Wait," one said, "this is too easy, it can't be more of them."

"More of what," I asked.

"More of the demons that came from the sky," he replied. "Who are you?"

"We are the future you," Chris answered, "and we are faced with those 'demons' you speak of."

"Then let us help you," the man said. "We have fought them."

"That's why we are here," I replied. "We need to know how to read your stone map."

"Who understands the most about maps," the man asked.

"I do," Heather said.

"Then I will tell you," he continued.

"How come she gets to know everything," Krissy complained.

"Because she's the smart one," Chris answered. The native took Heather and I over to Stonehenge and started explaining it. Meanwhile the others sat down. Some younger natives went over, probably about our age, and were hitting on Steph and Krissy. Steph stood up.

"Back off or I'll have my boyfriend beat you," Steph said.

"Whose your boyfriend," one asked.

"That one," she replied while pointing at Chris.

"Boyfriend?! What do you mean," Chris wanted to know.

"You're my boyfriend," Steph continued. "Right?" Steph winked at Chris.

"Yeah, right," Chris said. Then he muttered under his breath, "since when?"

"So you want to start something," the native asked.

"Wait a second," Chris said. "Do I know you?" The native

punched Chris right in the stomach. "Will people stop hitting me in the stomach," Chris screamed as he charged forward and knocked the native over. Heather looked over at them. Then she looked at me. She pulled me to the side. The native that was explaining the map looked to the chaos and was getting annoyed.

"If they screw this up, he won't tell us how to read the map," she said.

"What are you saying," I asked.

"Do something," she screamed at me. I ran over to where they were fighting. I broke up the fight between Chris and the native. The native stopped and looked at me.

"So you want to get involved too," he said.

"Not really," I said. "Why do you ask?" He clapped his hands and three more natives came over. "I suddenly see why you asked," I said. "Thanks for asking but I'll go sit over here and Chris you will too."

"Why, I want to have some fun," Chris said. "Don't back out, you beat the Master of Time."

"Now Chris," I said, "and that's an order."

"Well, we are a team and this is supposed to be a democracy like the United States so you don't have to be the dictator," he continued.

"I am the leader, just like the President, and he orders so I order," I replied angrily. "And if you don't sit over there with me and let your testosterone level die down we won't know how to read the map!"

"Ah, yes," Chris said, "I think I will sit this one out." We started to walk away but got jumped by the four natives. The elder native came over and told them to get away. Chris got up and started to run toward them but I grabbed him and held him back.

"I think we can go now," Heather said. "I know all I need to know."

"Do you know how to kill the force," I asked.

"Do you know how to kill four natives," Chris asked, "because I do." The natives started to taunt Chris.

"Stop it," I said, "let's go."

"To kill the force," the elder said, "just…" Just then there was a boom in the sky. Blobs of silver liquid started to fall from the darkness. "Never mind," he said. "Leave, they're back."

"On three," I said, "one… two…"

"Where's Steph," Chris asked.

"I don't see her," Heather replied.

"We need to go now," I said.

"You guys go," Chris continued. "I'll catch up."

"Now," I said with force. "We leave now as a group."

"But the whole group is not here," Chris replied.

"We sacrifice one for five," I continued. Heather looked at me in shock.

"You leave," Chris replied. "I'm going back."

"Can we leave now, please," Krissy asked in panic. "I'm not asking to go on three, just go." She pushed her button and left with William.

"I'm the leader," I told Chris. "And I say we leave now."

"Ok," Heather said as she grabbed my arm and pressed the button.

"What are yo…" I tried to yell but we disappeared. Chris started to run through the village yelling "Steph". He heard a response from one of the buildings and went in. He was immediately greeted by the four natives.

"Looking for her," the one asked. "Then you came to the right place."

"Just bring it," Chris said with a stern defensive voice. Just then one of the creatures busted through the roof.

"What is it," one of the natives asked.

"I don't know but get it," another answered. The four natives ran at it and attacked it but as soon as they touched it, they fell over dead. Chris pulled out a test tube from his belt and scraped up some of the residue from the ground. Then he picked up Steph and hit the button.

CHAPTER NINE

We arrived back in the present and went into the house. I stormed up the steps and into our room and Heather followed. "I can't believe you just did that," I yelled.

Back downstairs Amanda asked, "how did it go?" Krissy and William just looked upstairs toward the yelling. "So I see it went well," Amanda continued.

Back upstairs the argument was just beginning. "What did you want me to do," Heather asked. "We couldn't just leave Steph there."

"Yes we could," I answered with anger in my voice. "I made the decision. Remember I'm the leader and I make the decisions."

"You're the leader, but the leader of a team." Just then Chris appeared outside the house. He came in and heard the yelling so he came straight upstairs and barged in.

"Yeah, that's right," I continued, "I'm the leader of this team, just like you and Chris and Krissy were told before our first mission."

"That was the first mission," Chris butted in, "when we had no idea what we were doing and we needed guidance. Now we need to cooperate to get things done."

"Who asked you," I threw back. "You're the reason this is a problem in the first place. Since when do you have the right to tell me you're not coming back."

"Since I want to save lives," he answered, "not take them."

"I made a sacrifice so the rest of the team could live," I continued. Heather kept looking back and forth at each of us.

"Yeah, you made the sacrifice but I went and fixed it," he replied. "Just like I fixed your relationship."

"Don't get our relationship involved," Heather said sternly. "That has nothing to do with you or the team."

"Fine," Chris said, "I need to worry about the TEAM, not myself. That's what makes me more qualified as a leader than you. That's why I listened to Triton in Atlantis instead of you. He was more qualified to make those types of decisions than you were."

"This is all about you and your quest for glory," I pointed out. "Ain't it Chris? You are the one that wanted to stay and die in Atlantis, just for the glory. That's what happened today, just for the glory."

"Alright, that's enough," Heather finally stopped us. "There is no "I" in team and it doesn't matter who is the more qualified leader. What we need to do is to stop thinking about ourselves and what we think is good for the team and start asking the team!"

"Why are you taking his side," I asked.

"There are no sides," she answered. "We can't take a life to save ourselves. Don't you understand that? We said after our last mission that we were either in or out as a team. We decided that we were in as a team so that means during a mission we either all come out or all die in the process of trying. That also means we make decisions and agree on them as a team."

"Oh," I continued, "that's funny. Wasn't it that Chris was the only one that actually wanted to stay and save Steph?"

"Yeah," Chris answered, "because you stopped the team from doing so."

"Stop it," Heather said again. "This is it. You can't win, it was a stupid mistake. TJ you're right that he should have agreed with the team."

"Hah," I said, "I was right and you were wrong."

"Shut up," she continued. "Chris was right because we said we win as a team or die as a team, that means the whole team. We agreed that Steph was part of our team and so that promise includes her. And he held that promise by not leaving Steph behind. Now we need to put this behind us and worry about the evil force."

"I have to get Amanda to test something," Chris said to change the subject. "I'll talk to you later." He looked at me and walked away. I walked toward the door.

"Where do you think you're going," Heather asked me. "We are not through."

"Now what do you want to complain about," I responded.

"Actually," she replied, "I wanted to tell you that even though you made a mistake, I still love you. But I guess you can't say the same." She walked out of the room and downstairs. Chris was coming up from the lab in the basement.

"Chris," Heather said, "we need to talk."

"Yeah, sure," he said.

"I just want you to know that even though I took your side, I still want him as a leader. I don't like you trying to overthrow him."

"You're assuming that I want to overthrow him, but you're wrong. I just wanted to save Steph's life because that is the kind of person I am."

"So is TJ. He just wanted to save the rest of our lives."

"Yeah, I see that, after all his wife is in the picture, of course you come first."

"Don't start with the relationship stuff."

"And may I pinpoint that you said the rest of our lives. That means Steph too."

"But that meant risking my life and Krissy's life and William's life and to TJ that is unacceptable."

"But he said it was a sacrifice."

"Yes, for our lives."

"No, for your life. He only cared about you. He only said about saving our lives because we were standing there."

"Whatever. No point arguing now over something that already happened."

"I agree, but realize that his decisions are for your safety not for the safety of the team. So maybe you could talk to him. And for your information, I almost did die."

"How?"

"Remember them four natives, they died. I'll talk to you later about it, I have to get my test results." He ran back down to the basement. When he got down in the basement Amanda gave him the results. "Oh no, that explains it. How would I stop this?"

"I think I have an idea," Amanda said.

Later that afternoon Heather sat down with me outside on the balcony. I wouldn't talk to her.

"TJ, I talked to Chris earlier this afternoon," she started. Then she paused to make sure I didn't want to respond. "He said that he felt the decision you made in the past was only based on me. He said that your decision was to protect me and not so much the rest of the group. Is that true?" I just sat there and didn't acknowledge her. "Please, talk to me, I need to know." I still didn't even look at her. "I want to let you know that I love you. Did you hear me?" She placed her hands on my face and held my face right in line with hers. "Listen. I love you!" I just turned away and paid no attention to her. "I stood up for you. That's right, I told Chris to put himself in your shoes. I told him to think what he would do if he had the choice to loose one life to save the life of his wife, best friend, and cousin or to save one person by risking the others. I told him that I understand where you came from and that you are still the leader and I don't want that to change. Now I know you are probably not going to talk to me but I am still going to say what I need to say. I am your wife and I want you to treat me like that when we are at home. But when we are out on a mission I am your partner, not just your wife. That means that I am just another team member. If I have to die, if you have to make that decision to risk my life or Krissy's life, or Chris' life to make sure that the team either dies together or lives together, then do it. Don't let the idea of me being your wife influence your decision. You are the leader and you have to make a decision that is good for everyone, not just me. Now I know that is hard but I want you to try."

"I can't do that," I said. "I can't make the decision to kill you or Krissy or Chris or anyone else. But when it comes to killing five or one, I am going to kill one."

"So what happens if I was Steph," she asked. "What if I was the one that was kidnapped? Would you have decided to leave and let me die?" I walked away refusing to answer that question.

Out in the backyard Chris gathered up Krissy, William, and Steph. "Now," he started, "Krissy and I need to train you two. We need to see what abilities you have, and what abilities we can teach you." He started training Steph and Krissy was working with William. In the meantime, Heather hopped in the rental car and drove to Stonehenge. When she got there she started looking at the rocks.

"Ok," she said, "if this is the altar stone, then the sun should be there. It is. Ok, if this is the altar stone, then the moon should be there. It is. The twelve zodiac constellations should be there, there, there." She looked around. "Oh my God." She ran back to the car and drove home.

Back in training, Chris was laying on the ground with Steph standing over top of him with a staff across his chest. "Not bad for your first time," Chris said.

"I'm a natural," she answered

"Are you really," Chris asked. At the same time, William was mopping the ground with Krissy's head.

"So when do I get to fight for real," William asked.

"I don't know," Krissy cried, "but leave me alone." He let go of Krissy. Krissy walked over to Chris, still in the same position.

"William is in tip top condition, cheerio," Krissy said.

"Now your talking about Cheerios," Chris said. "Anything to talk about food." Then Steph straddled Chris to give more pressure and hold him down. Heather ran in breathing heavily.

"It's time. The sky is lined up with Stonehenge." She looked at Chris and Steph.

"So what," Steph said, "you want to kill us by sending us into battle without the proper training? I already had a near death experience, I don't need another one."

"Oh, yes," Heather responded, "and it looks like you two are training well."

"What do you mean by that," Chris asked.

"I've been in a similar position, but not while training. It's exciting isn't it," Heather answered.

"Yes, very," Chris responded. "But I thought it might be easier to get in this position while training." Steph stood up and looked at Heather.

"I hope you don't let your husband make the decisions," Steph said to Heather. "At least not for us anyway. I think you're safe."

"Maybe we should have left you there," Heather replied. "Then you would have had a truly stimulating experience."

"Why don't you two knock it off," Chris asked.

"Stay out of this," they both responded at the same time. I walked out and stopped to see what was going on.

"Chris," William said, "I guess they told you."

"Shut up," both Heather and Steph said at the same time. I walked out closer to where they were.

"Look who showed up," Steph said, "Mr. Leader."

"That's it," Heather yelled. She ran at Steph and knocked her over. Steph flipped her around. Chris ran over and pulled Steph off of Heather.

Heather tried to run at Steph but I grabbed her before she could. Steph wiggled free from Chris and attacked Heather. I lost control of Heather and they started slapping each other and rolling around on the ground. They continued to scream as they pulled each other's hair. Chris and I walked over and broke it up. I took Heather off to the side.

"Honey, relax," I told her trying to calm her down. "She's not worth it."

"You're right," Heather replied. "Besides, the sky is lined up with Stonehenge. It's time."

"Alright," I said, "we need to go to Stonehenge."

CHAPTER TEN

When we got to Stonehenge, the sky was getting darker. A lightning bolt struck the altar stone. A man appeared in soldiers gear. He looked at us. He had claws on the ends of his arms. The claws were like those of a crab.

"Are you going to try to stop us," he asked.

"Whose us," Chris asked.

"The Army of Cancer," he replied.

"Army, did you say army," Krissy asked fearfully.

"What do you want," Steph asked.

"What do we want? My dear girl," he said, "we, just like the other eleven armies, want to control the planet. Why? Because this is the last planet with life that we have not conquered. All other planets in this solar system had life, until we came along."

"So," Chris said, "let me get this straight. You and your army, along with the other eleven armies want to take over our planet because we are the only planet that you did not wipe the life off of."

"Exactly," he said.

"Thank you," Chris continued. "I was just making sure I knew the facts."

"Then you have to get past us," I said.

"You," the soldier said, "you pathetic group of young people are no match for my army. We wiped the strongest of the strong off the other planets. There is no way six "kids" are going to beat us."

"Hey we are not just normal people," Krissy said with confidence. "We are Americans."

"I'm not," William responded.

"Ok, all but those two," Krissy continued. "But I'll have you know…"

"Why don't you put your money where your mouth is," the soldier butted in. "Instead of talk, talk, talk, why don't you fight?"

"Let's go," Chris said, "I'm ready. I mean we're ready." He shot a bubble of energy at us and lifted us into the clouds. We landed in some type of room.

"This is the portal," the soldier continued, "each army has their own environment." Just then it turned into a beach by the ocean. He stood at the edge of the ocean.

"So," Chris said, "where is the army that you speak of."

"Patience is the virtue," he said. "Crabs are slow." Just then thousands of crabs came on shore. Chris started to laugh.

"Crabs," Chris chuckled. "You call a bunch of crabs an army. Don't make me laugh." The soldier laughed back at him. The crabs lit up and started to grow until there were thousands of soldiers that looked just like the guy that we met back on Earth.

"Remind me to keep my mouth shut next time," Chris said to me.

"No problem," I responded. "You should do that more often." Heather looked evilly at us. The soldier lifted his arms into the air. Three swords appeared in each claw.

"Let's give you some help," he said. He threw the six swords at us. I grabbed two, Chris grabbed two, and William grabbed two. I handed mine to Heather, Chris gave one to Steph, and William passed one to Krissy. I took my sword and ran toward the army and Chris followed. I started slicing soldiers but it didn't kill them. Some soldiers ran over to the other members of the group. I sliced one of the soldiers' heads off and it regenerated. Chris sliced one in half and it remolded back together. Steph sliced off the claws of one and it fell over dead. She grabbed the shield from it.

"Hey guys," she yelled, "slice the claws." Chris ran and sliced the claws off one of them. He grabbed the shield as it fell over dead. I was getting swarmed by a ton of soldiers.

"TJ, catch," Chris yelled. He threw me the shield and I caught it. A soldier swung at me and I blocked it with my shield. I sliced off its claws and threw Chris the shield. Chris sliced a few, killing them. Then the lead soldier stepped up to him. He knocked Chris' sword and shield out of his arms. Then he cracked Chris in the face. He clapped his hands and thousands of crabs came from the ocean to shore.

"Not more soldiers," Heather said in disgust.

"No, my dear girl," the soldier said. "These are true crabs to plague the Earth."

"And when the force is awakened," William started, "there will be more plagues and they will be more massive than those of Egypt. The Earth will be swept by the plagues of the armies and destroyed."

"How do you know this," Krissy asked.

"My mother," William answered. "My mother was right. The books that we read for years were true."

"So how do we stop the plagues," I asked.

"We have to kill the armies," William answered. Chris got up and ran at the lead soldier. He kicked each of his hands and the leader's shield and sword flew off into the distance. The leader picked Chris up with his claws. Then Steph and Heather ran over and each cut off a claw. The leader fell to the ground dead. Then the rest of the army fell also. We stopped, catching our breath. The plague of crabs disappeared before they could even cause any harm.

We fell back to Earth and looked at Amanda who was waiting for us at Stonehenge. "Mom," William said, "I want to apologize for not believing you. You were right." Amanda just smiled.

"Well," Chris said, "if the rest of the armies are like this, it might be a piece of cake to win this battle."

"This was the first and easiest one," Amanda replied. "It's only going to get more difficult."

"Great," Krissy said, "this was bad enough."

"When does the next army awaken," Steph asked.

"Tomorrow," Amanda replied. "The armies will awaken one by one, each day at midnight. There are twelve armies so there will be twelve battles over twelve days. You have until the last second of this year to defeat them. Once the new year is rung in, all armies left will become unstoppable."

"So we need to get sleep," I said.

"Let's head home," Amanda responded. We got in the car and drove home. Heather and I walked upstairs and went to bed. The others did the same.

We were awakened to the sound of explosions. I looked at the clock. It was 12:05 in the morning. "Get up," I yelled to Heather, "they're here." We jumped up and the others were coming out of their rooms. We ran out of the house. The lead soldier was standing outside.

"So these are the heroes of Earth," he said as he started to laugh. "I thought I would meet you at home. Why make you drive to Stonehenge to get destroyed?" Before we could respond he warped us up to the portal room. This time the room was a field. "We are the army of Capricorn," he continued. "But first the plague."

Back on Earth Amanda was standing outside her house. Just then meteorites started pouring down from the sky. She ran inside. London was being destroyed by gigantic meteorites collapsing buildings and setting others on fire. All around the world, the meteorites were falling. From New York, to Los Angeles, to Tokyo, to Cairo, to Munich, and so on. "And from the skies fall the Rings of Saturn," Amanda said to herself. "Capricorn unleashes the fury of Saturn."

Back in the portal I ran at the army. These guys were better at communicating than Cancer so I knew it would be more of a challenge. I sliced of one's head but that didn't kill it. I thought about how to kill a four legged animal type soldier. I sliced one of the soldiers legs and found that if you sliced both off they died.

"Go for the legs," I yelled. The others started slicing the legs. One ran at Heather and she tried to slice its head, but it ducked. Then she turned around and swiped her sword across its legs and it fell over dead. Krissy was taking her anger out on the soldiers. Steph was doing decent and William was a pro at sword fighting. Chris was taking his share at killing these soldiers. I thought that if I took out the leader that we could get rid of the army. I ran toward the leader and he sliced at me and cut my shoulder. I blocked his next swing with my shield. Chris came up from behind him and sliced his legs off. The entire army fell dead.

We warped back down to Earth and found it to be destroyed. "Oh my God," Heather said. "What happened?" Amanda was waiting for us outside the house.

"The meteorite shower finally stopped," she said. "The plague says that the fury of Saturn would be unleashed."

"How are meteorites the fury of Saturn," Krissy asked.

"They are from the rings of Saturn," Chris replied. "Duh!"

"I'll show you duh," Krissy said in fury as she started to storm toward Chris. I ran over and stopped her before she could get to him.

"Come on," Amanda said, "I'll make us all something to eat."

CHAPTER ELEVEN

Later that night, around ten, Heather and I were relaxing on the bed in our room. Heather looked at me and I smiled. "I don't feel good," she said out of nowhere, "I think I'm getting sick. It just came to me all of a sudden. I felt great before, but now I'm not feeling so hot. "

"So why don't you sit this battle out," I replied.

"I can't," she said. "We are a team, we all go, or we all stay."

"I think the rest of the team will understand."

"No, it was the promise we made to each other."

"Ok, I just don't like to see you sick." She cuddled closer to me and closed her eyes.

Amanda knocked on the door and came in.

"I made some dinner," she said, "I figured you were hungry because you haven't eaten since last night after the battle."

"Thanks," I said, "but Heather doesn't feel good."

"You can go," Heather said.

"No, we go as a team or stay as a team," I replied. She kissed me. Amanda smiled and walked out. She went back downstairs. The others were sitting at the table eating.

"So," Chris said to Amanda, "you seem to know about he plagues and stuff. What can you tell us?"

"Each army has a plague," she explained.

"So guys," Krissy butted in, "two down and ten to go." They all got up and left. Krissy continued, "we are doing good. Let's keep up the good work. We are the Time Warriors. We are unstoppable." Two hours later, we all met outside the house.

"Does anyone mind if Heather doesn't fight this battle," I asked. "She is sleeping because she doesn't feel good."

"Of course we don't care," Chris replied. "Why?"

"She said that we need to all go or all stay as a team," I answered.

"No that's fine," Chris continued. "We understand that she is sick."

"Then I won't wake her up," I said. We stood there and waited. Suddenly the sky opened and a soldier fell down. He was a human and he had a golden bow in his hands. He warped us up immediately. This time the portal looked like a regular forest.

"This is the archer," William said. The leader took his bow and shot an arrow of energy at the trees. He kept doing that. Then the soldiers of his army appeared from those arrows. "They have arrows of energy,"

William continued. I got my shield off my back and pulled my sword out of my belt. I ran at a group of soldiers. This time they were scattered throughout the woods.

"Split up," I said as I ran toward a cluster, "that's the only way." I ran at the group and they started shooting energy arrows at me. I blocked them with the shield but the force of the energy threw me backwards against a tree. "Wow," I said, "I can see it's not so easy anymore." Chris ran toward another group. They shot some arrows at him and he tried to slice them with his sword. That didn't work, they broke the sword.

"Oh great," he said, "I lost my sword." Steph climbed up a tree. Then she looked down on a cluster. She jumped down and kicked them in the face. She punched a few in the stomach and knocked them down. She grabbed a bow. When they stood up she shot them and the energy made the soldiers explode.

"Get a bow," she yelled, "that's how you beat them." I climbed up a tree and waited for a soldier to walk by. One came near the tree and I jumped down on him and he fell over. I grabbed his bow and shot him. He exploded. Then I heard Krissy scream. She was being held against a tree by two soldiers with one getting ready to shoot her. I shot the one that was going to shoot her. Then I took out the other two. I climbed back up in a tree and started shooting at every soldier I saw. Then one soldier jumped from the ground to the tree where I was.

"Holy shit," I cried. He kicked me and I fell backwards out of the tree. Chris was being overwhelmed by a group. Krissy was hiding in a tree shooting at the group that was after Chris. I didn't see Steph. I went to shoot the soldier that knocked me out of the tree but another soldier shot an arrow at me. I blocked it with my shield and flew backwards against a tree. Darkness quickly took over my eyes.

When I woke up our team was tied to the trees but didn't see Krissy. I wasn't tied to a tree for some reason. "Psst," I heard a voice. I looked up in the tree. It was Heather and she signaled me to be quiet. She had a bow in her hand. There were only ten soldiers left, including the leader. She started shooting at them. She took out five and then the leader saw where the arrows were coming from and started walking toward us. I ran behind the tree. She shot arrows at him but he was catching them. He started throwing them back. One hit her and she fell out of the tree. I jumped out and punched the leader in the face. He grabbed my neck and picked me up. He was getting ready to throw me. The soldier collapsed and we fell to the ground. I looked around to find Krissy standing there with a bow. I smiled at her and shook my head. The other four soldiers disappeared. I walked over to the other team members and untied them. We warped back to Earth.

There were fierce storms on the Earth so we ran inside. "And when the army of Sagittarius is defeated, the left over energy will release a plague of fierce storms from the planet Jupiter," William started. "The storms will flood all lands and burn all forests with the fierce lightning.

The storms will continue until all armies are defeated."

"So in other words," Chris replied, "the sooner we take out the other armies, the sooner we get rid of the storms."

"Yes," I said, "but if the rest only get harder, we are in some serious trouble." I looked at Heather. "What were you doing up there," I asked.

"I needed to help our team," she answered. "The leader warped me up there, but I was able to hide."

"What's next," Chris asked.

"I don't know," I answered. "But did you see how the first two were normal armies and this one had the power of energy."

"Yeah," Krissy said, "I did notice that. Does that mean that all of them have some kind of power?"

"I don't know," I continued, "but at least they stay in the portal. It would be very unfortunate if they got on Earth." Just then another soldier fell from the sky.

"It can't be time already," I cried. "We just got done."

"Yes," Heather replied, "but it took you that long to defeat the last one." The soldier stood there looking at us. He had a gold cloth at his waist and that was all. He had the symbol of a scale engraved on his chest.

"Libra," William said, "the Army of Libra." The soldier nodded his head. He warped us up to the portal. The portal was a platform like a see-saw. He opened his hand and had many little scales in it. Then he placed them on the ground. He put two fingers to each of his temples and closed his eyes. The scales grew into soldiers. Then he took his arms and lifted them into the air. He flung them forward.

Down on Earth, Amanda was standing in the kitchen doing dishes. A wave of psychic energy flew past her and made her dizzy. She fell over and hit the floor with a thud. The wave went all around the world knocking everything off balance. In Northampton, my mom and dad were sitting in the living room. Our cars had been destroyed by the plague of Capricorn. The wave swept through and they fell off their chairs. My brother was walking in the kitchen and he fell over. "What's happening," my mom asked. Back in England, Amanda was struggling to get up. When she got up she stood there.

"And when the Army of Libra is awakened," she started. "An unbalance will leave the world in chaos. It will knock buildings off their foundations and people off their feet. Headaches will rage and dizziness will increase danger. When the army is destroyed the unbalance will be destroyed also and harmony will return to the world." She rubbed her head because she had a headache. "Thank God for those kids," she continued.

Up in the portal we continued to battle with the army. I ran at one of the soldiers and he lifted me into the air with his psychic energy. He used it to knock my head around and give me a headache. Heather ran at another and he knocked her off balance. She fell to the ground and screamed in pain.

"These guys can play with our heads," Chris said.

"It hurts," Steph said. "I got a headache, more massive than I ever had."

"If we don't beat them quick," Krissy said, "I think my head might explode."

"But how," Chris asked. "We can't even get close to them."

"They like to make things off balance," William said, "and they are really balanced. Maybe we need to knock them off balance." I took that advice and ran at a soldier. I pulled my sword from my belt and threw it at his feet. He caught it with his psychic energy and turned it around and threw it back at me. I grabbed it and jumped at him. I swung the sword at his feet and sliced off his one foot. He fell off balance and turned back into a scale. I stepped on the scale and broke it. The others saw what I did and tried to do the same.

"Hey," Chris yelled to us, "this is a see-saw. Why can't we make it unbalanced? That should wipe them all out at the same time." We all ran toward one end of the platform. The soldiers ran toward us. The see-saw became unbalanced and they all collapsed back into scales. They started to slide off the platform. So did we but we grabbed on. Chris, William, and I pulled ourselves up and ran to the other side of the platform. It wasn't easy because it was almost vertical. When we got to the end, the platform leveled out and the girls climbed up. We warped back to Earth.

The harmony and balance returned and the headaches went away.

"You guys are doing great," Amanda said. "The armies didn't even make it out of the portal yet."

"What do you mean," I asked. "Can they actually get out?"

"Well, in ancient times they attacked Earth," she answered.

"Oh great," I said. "That means we better be careful not to let them get out."

"If they do, they are going to go after something that involves time," Amanda continued, "that's how the story goes. Did you ever hear the story?"

"No," I answered.

CHAPTER TWELVE

"The story," Amanda started, "is what got me interested in this topic. I heard it in school. I guess it is an English tradition, not an American tradition."

"Can you tell us the story," Chris asked, "it might help us."

"Sure," Amanda replied, "if you want. But William and Steph are going to have to help because I forget some of it. Here goes. At the beginning of time, when the big bang theory took place, the universe was created. Our universe was created and billions of stars and planets were scattered about in galaxies. Then something magnificent happened in our universe, but particularly in our solar system. That event was when life formed. It had never happened in any other universe, except the universe of darkness. The universe of darkness contained an evil force, if it was life I don't know, but that evil force did not like life at all. The force entered our universe and found it's way to our solar system. It found life on all of the planets in our solar system. The key strategy to the evil force is that it was able to create armies. The force created the Zodiac, the twelve constellations that rule our future. It sent the twelve armies down on every planet in our solar system. Every planet was destroyed and the life was killed by those armies except for one. The Earth. There was even life on the sun and moon and they were destroyed. The army that destroyed the life on the planet became the army of that planet and made sure that life did not appear again. For some reason, probably humans, the armies were not able to defeat the life on planet Earth. That is why today, Earth is the only planet that contains life."

"Yes," William picked up. "But the struggle doesn't stop there. These armies have and will appear every five thousand years or so until they defeat the Earth. Each time the life here on Earth must defeat them. If we were to move to other planets they would attack us there too, but only with the army that wiped the life from that planet. As you saw with Capricorn, it destroyed the life on Saturn, that is why it plagued us with meteorites from the rings of Saturn. Therefore it controls Saturn."

"The plagues will rage," Steph continued, "the armies will battle and the world will end in complete chaos. Right now we defeated the first four easy armies. There are still eight more to battle and they only increase in strength. The planets that have the stronger armies as their controlling army, had life that was able to battle that many armies. Unfortunately we do not know the order as of now because it has not been recorded."

"However, I am recording now," Amanda cut in. "Your team is the only force that can even try to stop this evil. You four were born to be the guardians of Earth. If you think about it, you are Earth's army."

"If you look to the sky," William continued, "you can see the twelve constellations of the Zodiac. Those constellations were formed by the force, it created a pattern in the sky. The ancient peoples on Earth saw those constellations and were in awe. The awe turned to fear when they were faced with those armies. That is why the Zodiac decides our future, and tells us what kind of person we are. Our ancestors may have been from the armies or from the planets the army beat. The story says that most likely, there were no humans on Earth until the armies attacked the other planets. The peoples of those planets fled to Earth for protection. The army that controlled that planet then governed those people from that planet."

"Wow," I said, "that's intense. I never knew it was that involved."

"Maybe that's what Scott was going to tell us," Heather replied.

CHAPTER THIRTEEN

It was just about time to fight the next army. I still couldn't believe that this war was that involved. And what was even harder to understand, our ancestors may have been from other planets. "So that means that the moon's life was the weakest, because it's army is Cancer and that was the first army and the easiest. Then it was Saturn with the Army of Capricorn. Next it was Jupiter with the Army of Sagittarius. And the last that we know was Venus with the Army of Libra," I said. "So what's next?" Just then a soldier dropped down from the sky.

"I am the leader of the Army of Aries," he said. "From the planet Mars, soon to be the planet Earth."

"Well I'm Chris," Chris told him, "an Earthling that is about to kick your ass."

"We'll see about that," he responded. He warped us up to the portal. When he set us down the army was already in front of us. They had a metal body with the head of a ram. They growled and snarled. The portal was a mountain with a lot of rocks.

"They look angry," Chris said. "I think they are a bit aggressive."

"That's what Aries is known for," William replied. "They are also very highly active and defensive when they don't get their own way. Lucky for us, they jump into situations without thinking."

"Go for the horns," I said, "that's got to be the weakness." I ran toward a soldier and tried to slice it's horns with my sword but it grabbed my sword and lifted me up. Then it swung me around and threw me down on the ground. I picked up a rock and threw it at the soldier. He caught it and whipped it back at me. I ducked and it missed.

"These guys are strong," I said. Heather ran at a soldier and tried to kick it but the soldier grabbed her foot and flipped her backwards. She fell on the ground and let out a cry. Meanwhile Chris was punching one in the chest. All it was doing was making Chris' hand really red because the body was made of metal. The soldier picked Chris up and threw him into the air. Chris hit the ground with a thud. Steph ran at one and kicked it in the back. The soldier quickly turned around and grabbed her by the throat. It held her up, choking her. Then it threw her backwards into a rock and she hit her head. William was slicing at the soldiers bodies. He cut off the horns of one and it fell over dead. He continued to do that. He was the only one of us not having a problem.

"Now I see why Mars had such a problem," Krissy said. She sliced off the horns of a soldier and it fell over. "Hah, hah, hah," she laughed in its face. Just then another soldier grabbed her and threw her. She landed on the ground and held her back in pain. I ran up behind the soldier that threw Krissy and cut its horns off. It fell over. One was chasing Heather with the sword that it stole from her. I ran up and cut its horns off. I took the sword and gave it to Heather. She sliced another soldiers horns off. Then a soldier ran up and swung a sword at us that he took from Steph. I jumped over it and so did Heather. Then he swung at our heads so we ducked. We jumped behind a boulder as it swung straight down at us. It cut into the boulder and got stuck. I took my sword and cut his horns off.

"Help," Krissy screamed as one of the soldiers picked her up. Chris ran over and cut its horns off and it fell over. He made sure Krissy was ok. Then he ran over to Steph because some soldiers were getting ready to attack her while she was unconscious. He swung his sword in a circle and cut all of their horns off and the fell over. Steph was waking up and Chris gave her his sword.

"Get the weapons," the leader yelled, "we are losing." They pulled out boomerangs that were made of metal and very sharp. One threw the boomerang at Heather and I but we ducked. Chris caught a boomerang as it flew at him and he threw it back and it cut off the horns of the soldier. He started to do that to the rest of them.

"This is easier," he yelled to us. I ran over and cut off the horns of a soldier and grabbed the boomerang and then I did the same to another. I gave one of the boomerangs to Heather. Chris gave a boomerang to Steph,

Krissy, and William. We all started throwing them at the soldiers while avoiding the ones that the soldiers were throwing at us.

"Now the plague," the leader screamed. Rams ran down from the mountain top and jumped out of the portal. They scattered across the world terrorizing the planet. They would knock people over and stab them with their horns. Amanda was fighting some off.

"They must be fighting Aries," she said. "Rams will plague the world coming from all the mountain tops. They will stab, charge, and trample all people sparing no one. They will eat all the crops and kill the forests. The Earth will run out of food." Meanwhile back in the portal, the battle was still taking place. We were down to a few soldiers. When we finally killed them they all disappeared and the portal returned to its normal state. The rams that were on Earth disintegrated and we warped back to Earth.

"This keeps getting worse," Chris said. "First we had two normal armies, then we had energy, psychic, and now strength." Amanda came walking out of the house.

"I found a book on the story," she said, "I must have bought it when I was a little girl."

"That was when the dinosaurs walked the Earth," William said.

"Don't say dinosaurs," Heather replied, "I don't like dinosaurs. I've had some bad experiences."

"Anyway," Amanda continued, "the book says that if the portal should open that the remaining armies would appear at once and scatter throughout the world attacking the biggest monuments that represent time."

"It's a good thing that hasn't happened," I said. "Let's be extra careful that it doesn't happen." The midnight clock rang.

CHAPTER FOURTEEN

"We are down to seven," I said. "We're doing good. We have seven more days to defeat the seven armies. A beam hit us and warped us to the portal. There was nothing in sight, just complete darkness. We started to walk around and explore.

"This is weird," Heather said, "it's midnight there should be an army."

"There is," William replied, "it's just being creative."

"What army would that be," Chris asked.

"The Army of Leo," Steph answered. Just then we heard a roar. We pulled our swords out and looked around. "They have very good leadership skills also," Steph continued. "And they like to show off."

"Great," Chris replied, "that's why they are playing tricks."

"Hey what's this," Krissy said. She was standing by a button that was lit up. The sign by the button said "push for next army."

"Don't push it," I yelled, "it's going to open the por…" Before I could finish Krissy pushed the button and a gust of air came. "…tal," I continued. "It opens the portal."

"Great," Steph continued, "you just unleashed the remaining armies on the Earth."

"Wait," William said, "when the portal is opened the fury of the armies will be felt on the great monuments of time around the world." As soon as he said that the walls lit up. We looked at the walls. One wall had Big Ben in England with the symbol of Pisces by it. Another had the Great Pyramid of Egypt with the symbol of Scorpio. Another wall had the Great Wall of China with the symbol of Taurus. The last wall had the Coral Reefs in Australia with a symbol of Virgo. Then we looked at the floor and it had a picture of the Statue of Liberty with the symbol of Leo. The ceiling of the portal had a picture of Time Square with the symbol of Aquarius.

"Wow," I said, "that's too easy. Chris you are Taurus and Steph you are Virgo so you two work together to get rid of those armies. Krissy you are Scorpio and William you are Pisces so you two work together to destroy those armies. Heather is Leo and I'm Aquarius so we will head to New York to take care of those two armies. Good Luck!"

Krissy and William just warped out of the portal because they had to head to London first. Chris and Steph used Chris' time device to go to Australia. Heather and I used our devices to head to New York City. Meanwhile on Earth, the planet was swept by an evil wind. Amanda knew the portal was opened. "Oh God," she said, "the Earth is dead." She knew that the armies were prepared around the world because the President told the countries to stay on high alert. But she also knew that our human armies were no match for the zodiac armies. "Now all the plagues will be unleashed at once," she continued to talk to herself. "Lions will roam the planet as if it were a giant African Safari. They will eat the livestock and other animals. Finally they will go after humans after they run out of food." Just then she heard roaring coming from every direction and screams of pain. "The world will freeze and another ice age will begin." Just then a cold wind swept by and a puddle of water on the ground froze in front of her. "Oh my God," she said, "this is just getting worse." She opened the book and read the other plagues. "With the army of Pisces," she continued, "the world will be put into a stage of darkness filled with nightmaric creatures. This is the plague of nightmares." Just then the electricity died and the world went dark. Creatures lurked around in the dark. Any creature that you saw in your nightmares became a reality for you. She read on. "When the Army of Aquarius is unleashed the Water Army of Poseidon will awaken from Atlantis and reek havoc on the world. The Army of Aquarius will have control of the water army." Just then puddles of Water came from the ground and formed into soldiers. She started to breath heavier. "This is not good. The awakening of Scorpio will plague the world with menacing scorpions. The stings will be deadly and they will swarm by the millions." She closed her eyes and prayed.

When she opened her eyes there were scorpions on her shoes. She screamed and ran inside. She sat by the window and looked out. Then she continued to read. "The Army of Taurus will bring back prehistoric creatures. Flying reptiles will plague the world and dinosaurs will meet humans in the survival of the fittest." She looked outside and saw large dinosaurs and flying reptiles. "I can't read on" she said.

CHAPTER FIFTEEN

William ran up to the police station in London. "Evacuate the city," William said.

"You think I'm going to evacuate the city because a kid tells me to," the chief answered.

"You need to," Krissy replied. "There's an army coming toward the city to destroy Big Ben."

"I still can't put the city into a panic just because two young kids tell me to," the chief continued.

"I am part of the United States Time Warriors," Krissy said.

"Still that doesn't give me a reason," the chief continued.

"The U.S.'s team isn't good enough for you," she replied. Just then they heard an explosion. They looked out the window and saw a t-rex destroying a building. Then they saw pterodactyls flying in the sky. The ground was frozen solid.

"Ok, ok," he said, "I believe you. Just make it stop."

"I think it's a little late for that," Krissy answered. "Just evacuate the city. She ran outside. "Oh my God," this is truly the end of the world. The t-rex looked over at her. She stood still because she remembered what happened last time. The police chief came out.

"How do you expect me to evacuate a city as big as London," he asked.

"I don't know but you have to do something, the army is going to be here soon," she answered. Then she heard something in the distance. She listened closely.

"March, march, march," she heard, "left, left, left, right, left, left, left, left, right, left." She looked and saw the Army of Pisces coming toward her. William ran out and pulled his sword out of his belt that he was keeping it in. They looked and saw that the army was made of normal soldiers but they had gills.

"Stab them in the gills," William said. They started running toward the army. Krissy and William started stabbing at the gills as they ran past. The soldiers were dropping fast.

"Halt," the leader yelled, "fight the kids!" They started to fight back. They were psychic, just like Libra so they had the same tactics, like using psychic wave to lift you up and giving you a headache. The police chief ran back into the station.

"Calling all police officers," the chief was saying over his radio, "evacuate the city." The police officers rode up and down the streets announcing that the citizens had to evacuate. There was a mad rush of people trying to get out of London. Krissy was running and stabbing the soldiers. Every so often they would lift her up with their mind and throw her into something. England's army showed up and they walked up to Krissy and William.

"Use swords or something to hurt their gills," William said. "That will kill them." The army started to do that.

A few hours later, the city was completely evacuated. Most of London's army was killed off. The city was destroyed, not many buildings were left standing. Krissy and William put on the fight of their lives and yet the army was still standing strong. The army went after Big Ben. They were set on destroying it. Krissy and William ran toward the giant clock. They went inside and climbed the steps to the top of it. They came out on top of the clock. The leader was standing there. He ran at William and knocked William backwards off the edge of the clock. Krissy screamed. William grabbed onto the edge but the leader didn't know that. He turned around and started walking toward Krissy.

"It looks like the Army of Pisces gets control of the Earth," he said. Krissy saw William climbing up.

"Yes," she replied, "it does seem that way. Doesn't it?"

"What," the leader said shocked, "your not suppose to agree with me." William ran up and stabbed him in both gills and the leader fell over.

The army below collapsed and the plague of nightmares vanished.

"You should know," Krissy continued, "nothing is as it seems. Especially with the Time Warriors. The sooner you learn that, the better." She ran over and hugged William. They pressed their watches to communicate with us.

"London is safe," William told us, "the Army of Pisces is destroyed."

"Great job," I said. Krissy ran down to the police station and told the chief that the city was safe for the citizens to come back. He wanted to wait awhile to make sure. William met Krissy at the police station.

"Now we go to Egypt," Krissy said, "to fight Scorpio's army." She hugged William again.

"Look at it this way," he said, "we only have one more army to worry about, the others have two armies left."

CHAPTER SIXTEEN

Meanwhile, while Krissy and William were on there way to Cairo, Chris and Steph were about to embark on their first battle. They were in Sydney, Australia. Chris was keeping an eye out for the army. Chris went into the police station. "I am from the Time Warriors," he said. "There is an evil army heading here and you need to evacuate the city."

"I need to call the U.N.," the officer replied.

"You don't have time," Chris continued, "that's what happened in London. The plagues are already here. You have dinosaurs walking around and it is exceptionally cold for Australia."

"Patience is the virtue," the officer butted in.

"You know," Chris replied, "I've heard that a lot and every time, something bad came from it."

"Listen," Steph said, "I am from London, I know what happened there. I don't want that to happen to these people. Now you have a choice, you can either do what we say and evacuate the city or, if you don't, feel the consequences of the United Nations when you were responsible for millions of casualties."

"Alright," he said, "when you put it that way, I don't have a choice." He signaled to his officers to have the city evacuated.

"Wow," Chris said to Steph, "talk about using force."

"I did what I had to do," she answered.

"Why would they be after the Coral Reef," Chris asked.

"They're not," Steph answered, "they're after the Sydney Opera House. That was in the distance in the picture."

"Tricky," he replied.

"They can't make it easy," she continued, "you should know that by now." Just then a t-rex came running by the police station.

"Get it," the police shouted. They all ran out and started firing at it. It turned around and roared.

"NO," Chris yelled as he ran out, "stand still!" The officers ignored him and the rex came down and grabbed them. It stepped on a few. Chris grabbed Steph's arm and pulled her off to the side. The rex busted through the police station. Then some water soldiers came running up the street. They were carrying a little girl. A swarm of scorpions ran from the sewer. Chris ran after the water soldiers. He threw the boomerang at them. They splashed to the ground. The scorpions flipped out because of the water and they ran back down into the sewer. Chris ran over and got the girl. He made sure she was ok and then took her to an officer. Then he saw ice on the ground.

"The army is here," he said to Steph. Just then women appeared.

"We are the Army of Virgo," the lead woman said, "prepare to be destroyed." They were dressed in blue outfits. She shot ice out of her hands at Steph. Steph turned to ice. Chris ran at the leader but she flipped backwards through the army. He grabbed his sword and started swinging at the army. All you had to do was slice them enough to kill them. He ran through the army and grabbed a bucket. Then he filled it up with hot water from the bathroom in the police station and threw it on Steph. The ice melted.

"Fight to the death," the leader yelled to the army. "Work in teams."

"We won't be able to beat them as a team," Steph told Chris, "they are to methodical. But they worry about meaningless stuff. Watch this." She walked up to one of the soldiers. The soldier was ready to attack her. "Your hair is very messy," Steph said.

"What," the soldier replied, "that can't be." She pulled out a mirror and looked. Steph grabbed her sword and sliced her head off. Chris laughed. He did the same by running up to the soldiers and getting them occupied by something else and then killing them. Australia's army came and Chris told them what to do. The battle continued all day.

Later that night, Australia's army was defeated and Chris and

Steph were still battling. The Army of Virgo was getting small. Australia's army decided to retreat. The Army of Virgo charged toward the Opera House. They used their ice to freeze the Opera House. Chris went up to the leader.

"How would you like to go out on a date sometime," he asked her.

"Really," she replied, "I never had anyone ask me before."

"No not really," he answered as he stabbed her through the heart. She gulped for a breath and then fell over. Steph quickly took out the last couple soldiers that remained. The power of Virgo was sucked up and the plague of the ice age disappeared. Australia warmed up like it was supposed to and the Opera House started to melt. "Mission accomplished," Chris told us, "we are off to China."

CHAPTER SEVENTEEN

Heather and I ran to the mayor's office in New York City. I walked in. The secretary stood up. "Welcome," she said. "Is there a problem?"

"Yes," I replied, "I need to have the city evacuated."

"I'll inform the mayor that the Time Warriors are here," she continued. She walked down the hall and into his office. We stood there. Heather came over to me and held my hand. The secretary came out. "The mayor is busy right now but he will speak to you in about an hour."

"We don't have that much time," I said, "it needs to happen now."

"Then you need to go talk to him," she replied. I walked past her and into his office. He stood up.

"I thought I told my secretary," he started.

"Just listen," I said, "I am the leader of the United States' Time Warriors. I need this city evacuated and I need it to happen now and as fast as possible."

"Look," he tried to say, "I can't evac…"

"In my book," I butted in, "can't is not a word. You will evacuate this city. No ifs, ands, or buts. Or else you will be sorry."

"Is that a threat," he asked.

"No," I answered, "that's a promise. Now evacuate the city as fast as you can."

"But," he started but I walked out of his office. I walked out of the building. Some water army soldiers ran past. I took out my boomerang and threw it at them. They collapsed. Then I saw a lion running down the street.

"We need to get to the Statue of Liberty," I told Heather, "as quick as possible." We started to run in the direction of the statue. The police were going up and down the streets announcing the evacuation. There was a mad rush of people trying to get out of the city. The dinosaurs were attacking people. The lions were also attacking the people. The bridges got overloaded with cars. There were accidents all over the place. We took a ferry across to the statue. When we got to the Statue of Liberty, the army was forming. They were soldiers with normal bodies but they had the heads of lions. The leader shot a ball of energy at a bridge and it collapsed with all the cars on it.

"Cut off their heads," I said. "That would be the pattern." The NYPD was there. Heather and I led some cops in a battle against the army. I started charging through the line and slicing the heads off. It was working, they were dying. Heather was doing the same. I saw the leader float to the top of the Statue of Liberty. "Keep leading the police force," I yelled to Heather, "I'll get the leader." I ran in the base of the statue. I kept an eye out as I ran up to the crown. When I got to the crown I knocked the window out and climbed up to the top. I didn't see the leader anywhere. I looked around.

"TJ," Heather screamed with a police megaphone, "watch out, behind you." I turned around and the leader knocked me backwards. He kept punching me in the face. I ducked and he missed. I kicked him in the stomach and flipped him over. He jumped up and shot a ball of energy at me. I stumbled backwards and off the statue's crown. I pulled my slingshot out as I fell and shot it up. It hooked on to one of the spikes and I pulled myself up. The leader was surprised to see me back. I pulled the sword out of my belt. Then I grabbed the shield off my back. He started shooting energy paws at me. I blocked them with my shield. Then I slashed at him. He backed up. I spun around and stabbed him in the stomach. He healed quickly and shot some more energy paws at me. I blocked them with my shield but they were strong enough to push me backwards. I went to slice off his head but he ducked and I missed. He punched me in the gut. I stumbled backwards and he shot an energy paw at me. It hit me and I flew backwards and hit the torch with a thud. He jumped down to the ledge that goes around the torch. He came stomping toward me. I flipped backwards and up to my feet. I ran around the torch until I couldn't see him anymore. Then I climbed up to the top of the torch. I lined the sword up with his head and jumped down on him. He turned around with a snarl and I sliced his head off. He fell to the ground. The army and plague of the lions disappeared.

I looked down at Heather and she was looking up at me. Suddenly she fell over and grabbed her stomach. "Heather," I screamed! I shot my slingshot over to the crown and climbed in the window. I ran down the steps and out of the statue as fast as possible. I ran over to her and propped her head up in my arms. The paramedics were just arriving. "Heather," I continued, "say something." I didn't get a response. "This means war," I said angrily, "someone is going to pay." The paramedics loaded her in the ambulance. I pressed the button on my watch. "Mission accomplished," I said, "but Heather is down. She is on the way to the hospital. I don't know what happened. I'll fight Aquarius by myself, I am one." The mayor walked up to me.

"Can I leave the citizens back in," he asked.

"No, there is another army going to attack time square," I answered.

CHAPTER EIGHTEEN

Krissy and William walked up to the pyramids in Cairo. They knew they didn't have to evacuate Cairo because it wasn't threatening the city, just the pyramids. "Inside," Krissy said. They walked in the entrance. They each grabbed a torch from the wall. They walked down the passage way and found a swarm of scorpions. They used the torches to light them on fire. Then some of the scorpions turned into soldiers. They were human soldiers with scorpion tails.

"Go for the tails," William told Krissy. They ran at the soldiers and started trying to slice the tails. The soldiers were too quick and turned before they could slice. Krissy ran up behind one and as she went to slice it, it turned into a cat.

"Yikes," Krissy said, "it changes shape." She sliced the tail off the cat and it turned back into the soldier. She went to slice him again and he turned into a bat and started flying around the room. She lit it on fire with the torch and when it turned into the soldier, she sliced the tail. The soldiers started throwing things around and knocking things over. Then, in an instant, they turned back into the scorpions and ran out of the room. Krissy and William followed them. They ran out of the pyramid but before Krissy and William could see where they were going, one stung William. He fell over.

"Oh my God," Krissy said, "the sting is deadly." She pressed the button on her watch. "Dr. Johnson," she said, "I need an anti-venom now." She held out her hand and a bottle of it warped into her hands. She gave him a shot of it and he just laid there. She left him laying in the sand. He was weak but he would live. She ran toward the center of the city. When she got in the center she heard screams. Then she saw the soldiers terrorizing the people. One took a young woman and stung her. Another was burning some homes. A group of soldiers turned into quick sand and people fell into it. Then they stung the people and killed them. Krissy pulled the sword from her belt and started swinging at the tails and killing soldiers. She pulled out the boomerang and threw it at some. That killed a few. The remaining soldiers in this area combined into a giant scorpion. It started destroying more buildings. Krissy ran out of the city. The scorpion followed.

"I am Scorpio," she said, "I must think like one. I want to be destructive and secretive. I can survive well. I got it." She ran into the desert. Then she pressed the button on her watch. "Dr. Johnson," she said, "warp me a bucket of water." She put out her hands and he warped her the biggest bucket he could find. She dumped it on the sand and quick sand was formed. The scorpion ran at her and fell trapped into the quick sand. She clapped for herself. Then the leader appeared in front of her. He knocked her backwards and she fell. She stood up and he punched her in the side of the head. She fell to the ground and held her face. He grabbed her by the hair and picked her up. He turned into a monster and growled. She screamed. She punched the monster in the stomach and it turned back into the leader. She got loose and punched him in the face. He tripped her and she fell to the ground.

"Now I have you beat," he said to Krissy, "you put up a good fight. Especially for a kid." Krissy got angry.

"Kid," she screamed in anger, "I'll show you kid." She kicked him in the face and then in the stomach. The leader stumbled backwards and William cut off his tail. He fell to the ground and disappeared along with the rest of the army and the plague of the scorpions. Krissy ran over to William and hugged him. Her face was bruised and he touched it. Then he kissed her. She pushed the button on her watch.

"Mission accomplished," she said. "We're coming to help." Just then something made their heads collide and they fell into unconsciousness.

"That's awesome," I yelled in New York City. Three more days and only two more armies.

When Krissy and William woke up they were in a strange room.

They were tied to stakes. They looked around and saw a man in a black suit that covered his entire body. "What do you want," William asked. The man did not answer, probably to conceal his identity. He held up their belts.

"Hey," Krissy said, "those are ours. We need them to warp." The man walked over and untied them. Then some guys also in black suits covering their entire body and face threw them out and locked the door.

"Looks like we need a flight to NYC," William told Krissy.

CHAPTER NINETEEN

Chris and Steph were at the Great Wall of China. They looked around and didn't see anything. Chris hopped up on the wall and searched the perimeter. Then he saw a mass of people walking toward the wall. It was the Chinese army. Chris and Steph greeted the commander.

"Wait for my command," Chris said. Steph hopped up on the wall with him. The army stood behind them making up about ten thousand soldiers.

"I don't see anything," Steph said as she looked at Chris.

"Just wait," Chris replied. "I can feel them." Just then the ground started to shake. From a distance over the hill came over a million charging bull soldiers. They had the bodies of humans with the heads of a bull.

"A bull has a heart of stone," Steph said. "You take out the heart and you take out the soldier. Understand?" The soldier nodded. They pulled their swords out.

"Fight to the death," Chris yelled to the armies, "or else the world will meet death. On my signal. Ready, charge!" The armies ran at the charging Army of Taurus. Chris and Steph pulled out there shields and stood on the wall. "We get the ones that make it past the armies," Chris told Steph, "brace yourself." They took a deep breath. As the soldiers made it to the wall they sliced at Chris and Steph. Chris and Steph blocked the soldiers' attacks with their shields. They stabbed the soldiers through the heart. Chris took out his anger on the soldiers. The armies battled for hours.

After hours of battling Steph and Chris were so tired they looked like they were going to fall over. The Chinese army was wearing thin. The Army of Taurus was dying out as well. Finally it came to the leader of the Army of Taurus. Steph fell off the wall in exhaustion. All of the soldiers were dead. Chris met the leader. The leader kicked Chris in the stomach and pushed him backwards. Chris fell on his back. He jumped up and ran at the leader but the leader moved. He spun around and swung his sword at the leader but the skilled soldier blocked it with his shield. Chris ran into a near by tower and climbed it. When he got to the top he waited for the leader to get up there. He hit the leader in the head with his shield and tried to stab him but the leader blocked. The leader cracked Chris in the side of the head with the shield and knocked him backwards off the tower and Chris landed on the concrete wall with a thud. The leader jumped down. The weight of the bull-like creature cracked the wall. The leader was snorting.

"Taurus rules," he said. Lighting struck the wood on the wall and lit it on fire. Midnight rung and it gave us two days to defeat the armies. "Yes," Earth belongs to the zodiac," the leader said. "Lord Taurus will rule Earth." Chris jumped up and kicked him in the stomach. He stumbled slightly backwards. Chris swung his sword at him and then stabbed at him but the leader just quickly blocked.

"You forget that I am one of the guardians of Earth," Chris replied. "I must die before Earth is yours."

"That is easily arranged," the leader continued. He punched Chris in the face and Chris fell backwards. Chris hopped up quickly and ran at the leader. The leader stuck his foot out and Chris stopped. He grabbed the leader's foot and spun him over and the leader fell. The leader jumped up and grabbed Chris by the throat and lifted him into the air. Then he threw Chris backwards into the tower and the tower collapsed on top of Chris. The leader lifted his sword into the air and started to swing it around. Then he saw a reflection of Steph running at him in it. He spun around and sliced Steph in the side with the sword. Steph grabbed her side and the leader pushed her off the wall. She hit the ground with a thud and a scream of pain. The leader laughed with an evil sound.

"I win by myself," he screamed with an evil tone of voice. "I didn't even need my army." Chris came running at him and he turned around and punched Chris in the face. He picked Chris up by the neck and threw him down on the ground. Chris laid there motionless. The leader lifted his sword into the air and went to stab Chris but stopped suddenly and grabbed his heart. Steph twisted the sword inside his body and he fell over. The plague of prehistoric creatures disappeared.

CHAPTER TWENTY

Meanwhile back in New York City, I was at Time Square engaged in a battle myself. I was battling the Army of Aquarius with the help of some U.S. soldiers. The problem, the Army of Aquarius had help from Poseidon's army. Heather was still in the hospital and I didn't know what was wrong with her. The armies battled for hours and hours. It was New Year's eve and I didn't sleep in six days. The Army of Aquarius was freezing everything and they had sharp blades of ice that they threw at our army and killed them with. I started fighting with some soldiers from Poseidon's water army. I remembered how to fight them from Atlantis. Suddenly, I collapsed in exhaustion and my sight went black.

Meanwhile Chris, Krissy, Steph, and William got back to the FBI offices in Washington, D.C. and sat with some agents. They didn't know how to help me so they didn't even want to try.

When I woke up the Army of Aquarius was finished and Triton was standing there. "Wow," I said, "thanks."

"You owe me," he said, "but I know you won't mind helping me if I need it. Anyway I had to fight these guys before." He nodded to me and disappeared. I got up from where I was laying and looked. Heather was there. She smiled at me.

"I figured you could use some help," she said, "so I called Triton." I ran over and hugged and kissed her. Then I pushed the button on my watch.

"Mission accomplished," I informed the rest of the group, "we're coming home." The mayor walked over to me. He shook my hand.

"Thank you," he said, "you saved the world and now we can celebrate New Years in Time Square."

"No problem," I said, "bring the citizens home." He contacted his officers to let the people back in the city. The crowds started to rush back into the city. Time Square was filling up.

"Do you want to stay for New Years," Heather asked.

"I want to go home and sleep," I answered. She laughed. They started to hand out bottles of water to the people in Time Square.

Meanwhile in Washington, Chris was sitting at a desk. "So we fought five in the portal," he said to himself, "and six on Earth. But we didn't meet the one we saw in the past. Oh my God." He jumped out of his seat. "Five and six is eleven, there is still one more." He looked at his watch and it said 11:00 p.m. "That's not good."

"And when the other armies fail," William started, "the toughest will arise." Chris pushed the button on his watch.

"TJ, Heather," he said, "we have a problem."

"Now what," I asked. Just then a few blobby, silvery things fell from the sky. "Does this problem involve blobby, silvery, things falling from the sky." I asked.

"That is the last army," Chris answered, "the one we saw in the past. Don't touch it. I had Amanda run a test and we found out that it is mercury. This is the Army of Gemini." Just then people in the crowd started falling over dead.

"Ask William why people would drop over dead from drinking water," I told Chris. I heard William in the background.

"And when the Army of Gemini arises, they will be made of mercury," he said, "and the plague they unleash will turn the freshwater to mercury and kill all life."

"Oh my God," Heather screamed, "we just murdered millions of innocent people." I took a deep breath. A cat came walking up to Heather. "Ohh," she said, "look at the little kitty."

"Don't touch it," I screamed. Then I sliced it with my sword and it turned into a silver blob and disappeared. "The army can shape-shift."

"We just made the biggest mistakes of our life," she said to me. "We let the citizens in without thinking. I can't believe this."

"What's worse," I continued, "we have less than one hour to beat this army and we can't touch it."

In Washington, Chris ran down to the FBI science lab where Dr. Johnson was now working since his lab was destroyed in the bombing. "Where can I get sulfuric acid," Chris asked.

"I have some here in the lab," Dr. Johnson answered. "Why?"

"The last army can only be beat by it," Chris answered.

"How much do you need," Dr. Johnson asked.

"As much as possible," Chris replied. Johnson led Chris over to the shelf that had the acid. He handed him cases of it. William, Steph, and Krissy ran down. They carried it out to Johnson's Porsche parked in the parking garage. "I am going to borrow this," Chris said as he turned the car on because the keys were already in the car. The others hopped in the car and Chris pressed his belt. He programmed in the New York bay, present day. They warped. When they got to the bay they hopped out of the car and unloaded the acid. He saw that the salt water didn't turn to mercury.

"I am going to dump this into the bay," Chris started to tell the others. "Then I am going to take the Porsche and get the army to follow me. I am going to drive the car toward the bay and hop out right before the car goes in. I will run as far from here as possible. The army will follow the car into the bay. Amanda told me that mercury, water, and sulfuric acid will give us the most spectacular firework show the world has ever seen. You three need to dump the acid in the bay and then get out of here." He hopped back in the car.

Heather and I had little energy left to fight. The army was destroying time square. The army took a bomb and threw it at Heather and I. We ran but it blew up and we flew into the Christmas tree near by. We just laid there. Then I heard it. "Hey," Chris yelled as loud as he could. "How about you try to do that to me?" The army turned and faced him. Then they took off after him at a fast speed. He ran and hopped in the car. He couldn't start it up. "Come on," he screamed. Finally, just before the army got to him, he started the car up. He drove off and the army sped up to follow.

Krissy, Steph, and William just finished getting the last of the sulfuric acid into the bay and started running in the other direction. "Pull out," I yelled into my communication device. "We can't beat them. Chris pull out." He ignored my command and continued his plan. He drove to the bay. Chris looked at his watch, he had ten seconds left. The ball started to drop in Time Square. I crossed my fingers and closed my eyes. He jumped out of the car. The car splashed into the bay. The crowd in Time Square started the countdown.

"Five, four, three, two,..." the crowd yelled. The army charged quickly into the bay and exploded. "Happy New Year," the crowd screamed. Flames flew into the air and it lit up the night sky.

"He did it," I yelled to Heather. "He actually pulled it off." We started to jump with the fireworks exploding in the background. Steph ran over and gave Chris a kiss and William kissed Krissy. They all wished each other a happy New Year. The water turned back into water. The rest of our group met us in Time Square. We all congratulated each other. I looked at Heather.

"That was one rough battle," Krissy said.

"Thank God for sulfuric acid," Chris said.

"That was the best plan I ever witnessed," Steph replied.

"What a firework show," William added.

"Heather," I asked, "what happened to you earlier?"

"Something that happened to me about four months ago. You'll find out in about five months," she answered and smiled. I just stared at her in shock. Then we just joined in the celebration to welcome the new year of fun, love, and more missions. Many more missions.

MISSION FIVE:
THE RETURN TO PARADISE

CHAPTER ONE

"**S**he is so cute," Steph continued as she handed the baby back to Heather. Heather came home from the hospital just days ago. We were blessed with a baby girl and we decided to name her Calandra, a favorite name of Heather's. Heather took Calandra to the crib in the living room. Then she came back out to the kitchen and turned the coffee pot on.

"They started on a new headquarters," Chris said. "They have been working non-stop because the government said they need it now." Heather and I haven't been updated because we have been living in Northampton and haven't been involved. We decided to rent a house in Northampton for the time being in order to get away completely. We decided we wanted to take time for our marriage and newborn daughter.

"They should be finished building it in the next few days," William replied, "then we'll move in."

"Then we can get back to work," Steph continued.

"They nominated Chris as the temporary new leader," Krissy said.

"Ain't I lucky?"

"Hey," Chris responded, "watch it."

"So do you have a job while you are on leave," William asked.

"No," I answered. "The government is paying us for the six months that we are out." Heather got six coffee mugs from the cabinet and poured coffee in each of them. Then she handed them out.

"So what are you going to do for the next six months," Krissy asked. "Won't you be bored?"

"I'll be watching Michael," Heather responded. "He's my best friend's son."

"And I'll be looking at the findings of the Atlantis team to decide if they really found Atlantis or not," I told them. After we finished drinking the coffee Chris, Krissy, Steph and William decided to leave.

"Thanks for dinner," Krissy said as she gave Heather a hug.

"The baby is so cute," Steph said as she hugged Heather and I.

"Take care," Chris said to me as he shook my hand and then gave Heather a hug. William shook my hand and gave Heather a hug.

"Thanks for everything," he said They walked outside to the car. Chris got in the driver's side. Steph got in the passenger side. Krissy and William hopped in the back. Chris rolled down his window.

"Be careful heading back," I said.

"I will," he replied, "and I'll let you know if another mission comes up."

"Yeah, thanks," I answered. "Just remember, if you need me, call me. I'll be back in six months otherwise. Good Luck!" They backed out of the driveway and disappeared down the road.

I walked back in the house where Heather was cleaning up in the kitchen. I went in and started to help. "That was a nice visit," she said.

"Yeah," I replied.

"They'll be fine without us," she continued. "After all, they probably won't even have a mission."

"I know, but I still worry."

"If they don't have a mission," she replied, "how can they possibly get in trouble?" I gave her a look that told her I was saying "think who we're talking about."

CHAPTER TWO

On the way back to Washington D.C. they started talking. "It might be nice to go on a mission without those two," Chris said. "It won't be so controlling."

"Yeah," Krissy said, "instead of listening to the good leader and not getting killed, we'll have to listen to an idiot."

"You do," Chris replied, "not me."

"Ha ha, funny," Krissy commented.

"Now that we are a team," William said, "why don't you tell us how this team really started?"

"Good idea," Chris replied. "This team started when we were in high school. We had a guest speaker from the government talk about time traveling in our physics class. TJ asked how we could go about getting involved and the guy gave us his contact information. We got support from our parents, trained a few weeks, and, after we graduated, we entered the state competition for Pennsylvania. Each state had a competition with the winning team going on to nationals. The winning team of nationals became the Time Warriors. Obviously we won and we got to test the time machine." Krissy butted in, "I'll take it from here." Chris shook his head. "The bad thing was, the runner-ups had connections with the government and they were not happy. So they ended up messing around with the time machine and getting us stuck in time. Then, when they came to 'rescue us' they ended up trying to kill us instead. However, we beat them and used their time machine to get back to the present."

"That is the summary of a novel," Chris cut in. "It was only after long battles in a nightmarish world that we got to return home. We had to deal with the dinosaurs and the other team. Then when we returned they made us a new government team. When they opened the time traveling concept to the public, we had to track every movement. Then came Atlantis, the future and a time war, and then England fighting the armies with you."

"It must have been cool to see the dinosaurs," William said. "Wow, I could only imagine."

"Yeah," Steph agreed, "live, breathing, walking prehistoric creatures."

"You forgot eating," Chris responded. "Dinosaurs like to eat."

"Yeah," Krissy continued, "it's not really cool when you're running for your life."

"Oh come on," William replied, "it couldn't have been that bad."

"You weren't there," Chris argued, "you don't know."

"But I want to find out," William answered. "Take me back to see the dinosaurs."

"No way," Chris screamed without thinking.

"Oh come on," Steph helped William.

"No," Krissy helped Chris. "It is too risky. We know, we were there."

"What will it hurt to go back for ten minutes," William asked. "That is just enough time to get a good look at some dinosaurs."

"What will it hurt," Chris answered with a question. "Nothing is that easy. Something is bound to go wrong."

"Oh come on," Steph cut in. "Are you dinophobic?"

"Yes," Krissy and Chris yelled at the same time.

"You big babies," William continued.

"Look," Chris said angrily, "I was there. I saw what happens and I will not go again. End of story!" When they got back to Washington it was late in the night. Chris and Steph offered William and Krissy a place to stay. They agreed and they all went to bed.

CHAPTER THREE

The next morning when I woke up, Heather was up with Calandra. I went downstairs.

"Good morning," Heather said.

"Morning," I replied. We didn't fight as much now that we were on break from the team.

"I offered to watch Michael," she continued.

"Ok," I replied, "I am going to get some work done on the Atlantis findings."

"Sounds good," she said. "Don't forget that Calandra has a checkup this afternoon." She gave me a kiss and handed me Calandra. "I'm going to take a shower before Michael gets here," she told me. "Can you feed Calandra?"

"Sure," I answered. She went upstairs to take her shower. I went into the kitchen and warmed up a bottle. About fifteen minutes later, Heather came into the kitchen. She took Calandra from me and put her in her crib. The doorbell rang. Heather answered the door and it was Natasha with Michael.

"Thank you so much," Tasha thanked Heather, "the babysitter went on vacation and I couldn't find anyone else."

"You're just lucky that I had a baby," Heather replied, "or I wouldn't be on break. Plus, he's no trouble at all." Michael was normally very well behaved.

"Well he can be a troublemaker," Tasha continued, "so I brought his favorite dinosaur movie. He just loves dinosaurs."

"Ohh," Heather said hesitantly, "that's good he can watch it."

"Just make sure either you or TJ watches it with him," Tasha replied, "he gets scared."

"So do we," Heather said with a smile. Tasha laughed, thinking it was a joke, but Heather was not kidding. The sight or sound of a dinosaur on TV sends us into flashbacks, at least as of late. Tasha left and Heather cleaned up the house. Then she took Michael and Calandra outside. Meanwhile, I got my shower and started working on the Atlantis findings. For lunch, Heather ordered pizza for her, Michael, and I. After lunch, Heather took Michael and Calandra to the playground while I made some phone calls to the company in charge of the Atlantis research.

"Good afternoon," the woman answered, "this is Atlantech Research Company. Can I help you?"

"Yes," I replied, "my name is TJ and I am the leader of the Time

Warriors. I have been investigating the findings your company sent to me because I was in Atlantis."

"Oh yes," she said, "I remember. What did you find?"

"Well," I told her, "it doesn't look like Atlantis to me. In fact, a lot of the underwater structures that are in the picture, have no resemblance of the buildings in Atlantis."

"Oh," she replied disappointedly, "that's bad news. We will need a report from you though so if you could fax that over to us as soon as possible."

"I'll get working on it," I told her. "And tell your team to try looking around the Bermuda triangle."

"Why would you say that," she asked.

"Oh, I don't know," I answered, "it's just a hint. Have a wonderful day." I hung up the phone and started typing up the report.

CHAPTER FOUR

"This is our new building," Johnson told the team. He pointed to a large building made of pretty much all glass windows.

"Wow," Chris said, "this is awesome."

"Wait until we go in," Johnson responded. He started walking toward the door. The door was automatic and it opened at the first sign of movement. They walked in the building. Inside was a huge lobby with a marble floor. The pillars in the room were made of marble also. There was a huge gold chandelier hanging from the middle of the room. Basically it looked like a five-star hotel lobby.

"Unbelievable," Krissy gasped. There was a big office in the middle of the room.

"That's where the secretaries are stationed," Johnson told the team. Downstairs in the basement is my lab and office. This is the main floor and the elevator reads 'lobby'. On the first floor, Krissy and William have their offices. The offices look the same as the old building, pretty much plain. Also on the first floor is the Library of History and the Library of Food. William is now the historian of the team and Krissy is the chef. On the second floor, Chris and Steph have their offices. Also on the third floor, there is the Library of Criminal Justice for Chris, who will be in charge of developing time traveling laws. And then there is the Library of Languages, for Steph to master the language of the time period you are in so that you will be able to communicate with the natives. Finally on the third floor is where TJ and Heather's offices are located. The Library of Science for TJ and the Library of Psychology for Heather are also located there. There is also a babysitting department for Calandra and an indoor playground. On the roof there is an outdoor playground. And on each floor there is a mini-lobby and a snack room. On the ground floor is the conference room where you will meet to discuss missions. The equipment room is in the basement with my lab. There is a cafeteria on the ground floor as well. And that is about it."

"Well," Chris picked up control of the conversation, "then we should explore our new offices."

"That sounds great," William cut in, "we should go exploring." Chris looked at him. "The past," William mumbled. Chris shook his head. They walked away in a group.

"Please Chris," Steph begged. "Why can't you take me?" She gave him a puppy face.

"Don't even think about it," Krissy added. "There is no way."

"Oh come on," William said, "take me there."

"How can we refuse," Chris asked Krissy. "After all Steph is my girlfriend and William is your boyfriend."

"TJ would kill us," Krissy replied. "Plus you have no idea what you are getting yourself into."

"That's the point," Chris added. "No TJ, no Heather, lots of risk and fun."

"You can't lead us on a mission," Krissy told him, "you don't know what to do."

"Sure I do," Chris responded, "I would lead better than TJ. After all he saves his wife and cares nothing about us."

"Come on," William said to Krissy.

"Please," Steph begged.

"I don't want to do this," Chris continued, "quite frankly, I'm scared. The point is this is our chance to go on a mini-mission without our dictators."

"Alright," Krissy screamed, "I'll go. Talk about peer pressure. But only for ten minutes."

" Exactly, but we have to get out of here without Johnson seeing us," Chris told them. They started to walk down the hall to the elevator. They would take the elevator to the basement to get the belts. Just then Johnson walked off the elevator.

"Where are you four off to," he asked.

"We're going to…" Krissy started.

"We're going to TJ and Heather's," Chris butted in.

"Oh," Johnson said, "I thought you just got back."

"We did," Steph answered, "but I forgot something and we all decided to go back."

"Ok," Johnson replied, "I'll see you when you get back."

"Right," William responded. Johnson continued to walk down the hall.

"You two are really good partners," William told Chris and Steph.

"Yeah," Krissy continued, "you're almost as good as TJ and Heather. Not!" They took the elevator down to the basement and grabbed the belts that were there.

"Hello," Johnson yelled as he walked down the hall. "Are you still here?"

"Hurry," Steph yelled to Chris. They pressed the button and right before Johnson walked in the room, they were gone.

CHAPTER FIVE

When the team landed in the past, they ended up in a tree. "Don't you think we had enough experience with trees," Chris asked. They were hooked on the branch by their belts.

"See," William said, "this isn't so bad."

"Yeah," Steph replied, "if we could only get down to see some dinosaurs." Just then they heard a thud and a roar.

"I don't think we need to get down to see dinosaurs," Chris said. "I think we're about to see one." The trees started moving. The ground was shaking. Just then the large, predatory dino that we met before came to the tree and started sniffing around. Then it roared.

"Stay still," Chris said. The dino started to sniff Steph. Steph screamed and let go of the belt and fell to the ground. She scurried to her feet. The dino put its head down down to follow Steph. William quickly dropped to help Steph. Their belts were on the branch.

Steph ran off into the woods. William stood there shaking and whining. The dino ran over toward where Steph went. Chris let go of the belt and fell to the ground.

"Hey," Chris screamed. The dino turned around and looked. "Run," Chris yelled to William and he took off. Krissy fell from the branch leaving the belt behind. She took off and then Chris did. The dino didn't follow. He was interested with what was in the tree. He threw his head upwards and it hit the branch that the belts were hanging on. The branch broke with the impact and the belts fell to the ground.

"The belts," Chris screamed in panic. The dino looked over at him and started walking toward Chris. He stepped on the belts shattering them to pieces.

"Ten minutes," Krissy said. "No problem, ha. There is always a catch." The dino heard something moving in the woods and walked away. Chris ran over to the belts and picked up some pieces.

"Remind me to never, ever go on a ten minute trip," Chris said.

"I'm with you," Krissy replied.

"It can't be that bad," William said.

"Yeah," Steph continued, "Dr. Johnson will help us."

"Too bad, he doesn't know we left," Chris answered.

"Yeah," Krissy cut in, "neither does Heather or TJ, the good leaders."

"This is not my fault," Chris replied quickly.

"I know," Krissy answered. She looked at William. He just shrugged his shoulders.

"Now how do we get home," Krissy asked.

"Beats me," Chris answered. "I'm not as smart as TJ to figure things out like that."

"Yeah," Krissy replied. "After all, it's not like we have Einstein as a leader."

"Hey," Chris replied.

"Look," Steph butted in, "we can't fight. You two have been here before. Where did you stay last time?"

"We set up a camp near a waterfall," Chris answered.

"Then let's head to camp," Steph replied.

"Sounds like a good idea," William continued.

"So did the ten minute trip," Chris answered. "Nothing is ever a good idea. There are a lot of carnivorous dinosaurs that don't live far from camp."

"So let's hunt the dinos," William said. "They'll make a good dinner. They taste like chicken."

"Actually," Chris replied, "you're not hunting, you're being hunted. And they think you'll make a good dinner. We'll taste like chicken to them."

"So they eat meat," Steph said to make sure.

"Yeah," Krissy answered, "that is what he meant by carnivorous. Duh!"

"Sorry that I don't know all the big words," Steph replied.

"And we don't even have equipment," Chris continued. "We have nothing, and no one knows about us being gone."

Back in Northampton I walked into the kitchen. I saw a light flash before me and I was suddenly back on our first mission. I was up on the cliff. Then I saw a dino run out from the woods. I jumped up on the counter thinking it was the edge of the cliff. Heather walked in. I saw, in my mind, the dino run at me. I jumped. "TJ," Heather screamed!!! I jumped through the window shattering it. I landed on the ground and laid there bleeding. "Oh my God," Heather cried, "he went psycho." She ran out the kitchen door and came over to check on me. I was screaming and kicking because I was still in the flashback getting eaten by the dino. She slapped me and I snapped out of it. "Can I ask what you were doing," she said. I got up and looked around.

"I must have had a flashback," I replied. "I was getting attacked by a dino. It was the one that attacked us in paradise." We went inside and Calandra was crying. Heather left the kitchen to check on Calandra. I got some paper towels and started cleaning myself up. Then I got bandages and wrapped the cuts.

"We have to take her for her checkup," Heather said when she came back in. Natasha came in and picked up Michael. We hopped in the car and drove to the doctor. On the way to the doctor's office I was thinking about why I would have flashbacks all of a sudden.

"Something just isn't right," I said to Heather.

"What do you mean," she asked.

"I don't understand why I'm getting flashbacks now, so long after."

"Dr. Johnson said they could come at anytime."

"Yeah, but it just doesn't make sense. The littlest things are setting them off." When we got to the doctor we checked in. There were a lot of people in the waiting room and Heather looked at me. She knew as well as I did that we didn't exactly blend in. We were from Northampton, but we were celebrities. The people stopped what they were doing to look at us. They had the news on in the waiting room.

"Good afternoon," the newscaster said, "this is a news update. People around the Lehigh Valley are preparing for a fierce storm." I looked at Heather and then back at the screen. "According to our reports there is a fierce thunderstorm that could be carrying tornadoes making its way here to the Lehigh Valley. Radar indicates that it should arrive sometime in the early evening hours. Watch the news at 5:00 p.m. to find out how to prepare. That is all we know for now, watch the news at five. Have a great day!"

CHAPTER SIX

Meanwhile, back in the time of the dinosaurs, the team was making their way toward the campsite. "I think this is the way," Chris continued.

"Oh, that's great," Krissy responded, "you don't even know where you are going."

"Shut up," Chris replied, "just shut up. You are not helping." Chris stopped and listened. "I hear the river." He ran toward the river. When he got to the banks of the river he stopped and looked up and down stream. He realized that camp was just around the bend upstream. He started to walk and the others followed.

"If only TJ was here," Krissy continued complaining, "he would actually know what to do. See he studies the topic before he goes barging in. That's why he doesn't get us killed." Chris stopped walking and turned around. He gave Krissy a weird look.

"Did I get you killed yet," Chris asked.

"No, but…," Krissy tried to respond.

"Then shut up," Chris continued. "When I get you killed, then you can complain to me. Until then SHUT UP!!!"

"But I can't complain when I'm dead," Krissy said.

"I know," Chris answered, "that's the point."

"Well…," Krissy started.

"If you don't shut up," Chris cut in, "you will be dead before we make it to camp." Krissy stuck her tongue out at him when he turned around.

Meanwhile back in Northampton, we were still sitting in the waiting room. I was getting annoyed with the wait. Finally the nurse came out and called us back to the room. The doctor came in. He shook my hand and Heather's

"So, this is Calandra," he said, "that's an unusual name. Is she named after anything in particular?"

"No it is just a name that Heather liked," I answered.

"Oh," he continued. He started to examine Calandra. "What happened to you," he asked me.

"I had a flashback of our first mission," I replied, "and I jumped through the kitchen window."

"Ouch," he said, "you need therapy."

"I already had debriefing," I replied. "I think the government knows what they are doing."

"Ok," he answered in defense, "I can't step in against the government." He continued to examine Calandra. Heather just shook her head at me.

Back in the past, the team got to camp. Chris sat down on the rocks nearby. "This looks a bit different," Krissy said. "I don't think this is the exact time we were here." Steph walked over and sat down next to Chris.

"So far so good," William said, "there haven't been many dinosaurs."

"Jinx us," Chris said, "if that's what you are going for, say it again."

"Hey," Krissy replied, "chill out, you're getting worse than TJ."

"Yeah," Steph continued, "you flipped on TJ before, now you are just as bad. Or is it that you are seeing that being the leader is not that easy? Is it that you want the team to be safe? Do you care more about our welfare than anything else?"

"Shut up," Chris snapped. "I am not like that. I am not going to put Steph before the team. I am the leader and even though she is my girlfriend, I can't favor her."

"You will eat those words," Krissy said, "just like TJ did. He said that until it came down to a life and death situation for Heather. You will do the same, just wait and see."

"I will not," Chris said angrily. "TJ is a bad leader, he wants all the glory. He wants to look good for the government. You don't see this, but I do. He is more concerned with Heather than any of us. Heather knows that. They should stay off the team, we don't need them."

"You don't mean that," Steph said sadly. "Chris, say you don't mean that."

"I do," he yelled. "I mean it with all my heart!" Steph got up and walked away. Krissy and William walked over to the edge of the river. Chris just shook his head in disgust.

Back in the present, we were still with the doctor. "Well," the doctor said, "everything seems to be normal. She is a healthy little girl. She should be, she has great parents. All right, you are all set to go." We got up and walked out of the office. We paid for the visit and made our way to the car. The sky was really dark and cloudy.

"We are going to get a storm," Heather said, "and it is going to be a wicked one." We got in the car and drove away. When we got home it was raining. Heather ran in the house quickly. I grabbed Calandra out of the back seat and ran in the house. "You do realize you left the window open," Heather said. "The one that you broke."

"Oh yeah," I said, "I forgot about that."

"You don't think someone snuck in," Heather asked, "I'm scared."

"No one came in," I replied. I put my arms around her. Calandra was sleeping so I took her upstairs and put her in the crib. Then Heather and I sat down on the couch and watched TV.

"What about the follower of the Master of Time," Heather asked. "You don't think he is after us."

"No," I answered, "don't worry about it." I put my arm around her. She got up and went into the kitchen. The storm was really bad. There was lightning. Just then lightning struck nearby and the lights went out. Heather walked over to the window and looked outside. I lit some candles in the living room. Heather stuck her head out the window and suddenly there was a flash of light. She was back with the dinosaurs. It was night and she saw a dino lurking in the dark. Just then she snapped out of it and stood there. Then she imagined the dino sticking his head through the window and snarling at her. She screamed and I ran out to the kitchen. She was against the table shaking. I went over to the window and looked around. I didn't see anything. I walked over to her and tried to calm her down.

"What is it," I asked.

"I saw a dino come through the window at me," she replied. "I must have had a flashback." Then we heard a crashing upstairs in the baby's room. We ran upstairs and into her room. "Oh my God," Heather screamed, "the baby!"

CHAPTER SEVEN

The team was sitting around camp when they suddenly heard something moving in the woods. Chris looked and saw a pack of dinos walking around. They were different than the last ones. They were a little larger and looked a lot more vicious. They stood about seven feet tall and their huge teeth were showing over their bottom jaw. The dinos looked over and saw Chris and immediately ran at him. William ran at one and kicked it in the side of the head.

"No," Chris yelled, "don't do that." The dino shook his head and ran at William. William jumped in the river and swam to the middle so he was far enough from shore. A dino saw Steph and ran over at her. It snapped at her and she screamed. Chris ran over and kicked it. The dino chased Chris up a nearby tree. The dino called for the others to help at the tree and they all ran over. "Jump in the river," Chris yelled to the others. The dinos tried to jump up at Chris but he was too high. Then they heard something coming from the river and ran away. "Get out of the river,"

Chris screamed to the others, "something is there. It spooked the raptors." Suddenly a huge crature popped out and roared. It had an extremely long neck. Chris jumped down from the tree. The others swam to shore but opposite of camp. The creature chased the team out of the river. When they got out of the river, they were met by the giant predatory dino. The river creature decided to stay in the water.

"William," Krissy screamed, "come back." The team, with the exception of William, climbed a tree. The dino continued to chase William through the woods and he disappeared out of sight. Krissy and Steph climbed down from the tree. Chris was swimming across the river to meet them. "We need to get William back," Krissy told Chris.

"We will," Chris replied as he met them on shore. "But the problem I see is that the creature in the river was not here last time. So that means that there could be more new dinos that we never met with."

"Probably is never the way it is," Krissy responded. "There are definitely more new dinos."

"If only we wore our watches and outfits," Steph said. "We would've been able to contact Johnson." They walked in the direction that William ran. They eventually were walking uphill and eventually made it to the cliffs overlooking the waterfall.

"We were here before," Chris said.

"Yeah," Krissy replied. "And we jumped down there last time. I am not doing that again."

"Help," someone screamed! Chris knew immediately that it was William. He ran over to the edge of the cliff and William was hanging there. "Help me," William said. Chris stood there thinking what to do.

"Help him," Krissy screamed at the top of her lungs!

"Quiet," Chris said. "We don't want a dinos…" Just then there was a roar from the woods nearby. A giant meat-eater, one they had never seen before, came running out into the open field. Krissy backed up slowly and fell backwards off the cliff. She grabbed onto a root near William and they hung there. The dino ran toward Steph and Chris. "Jump," Chris yelled to Steph. He grabbed her arm and they jumped off the cliff. They screamed the whole way down. They floated down the river. Krissy and William were still hanging there. They slipped off the roots and fell to a ledge below. There was a cave in the wall. They walked in and looked around. A ton of little dinosaurs ran toward them and started biting them. Krissy screamed in fear and pain. The dinos were about two feet high but vicious. William started shaking them off but they just jumped back on. Krissy was trying to kick them but they just jumped on her. Krissy and William ran out of the cave and jumped off the cliff. When they hit the water the dinos let go and tried to swim to shore. Krissy and William floated to camp where Chris and Steph were just climbing out of the river.

"We need to make some tents," Chris told the team. Chris took sticks and leaves, just like last time, and constructed a tent. Then Krissy did the same. It was getting dark and they were hungry. "Let's go fishing," Krissy said to William. Krissy led William to the river while Chris started banging rocks together over a pile of leaves and twigs to start a fire. He finally got sparks and the fire ignited the material. Krissy and William brought four small fish up to camp and cooked them. They ate and then went to bed. Chris and Steph slept in one tent and Krissy and William in the other.

CHAPTER EIGHT

Meanwhile while they were doing all of that stuff during the day, at home Heather and I were in Calandra's room. "The baby," Heather was freaking out.

"What about the baby," I asked.

"She's dead," Heather replied and started to cry. I looked at the baby laying in her crib and looked around the room. The crashing sound we heard was caused when a shelf fell off the wall. The baby was fine but Heather insisted that she was hurt.

"The dinos got her," Heather continued. "They destroyed the room and killed Calandra."

"She is fine," I kept telling Heather. "She is laying right there in the crib asleep." Heather must have been having another flashback. I walked over and shook Heather to get her out of the daydream. I walked over and picked Calandra up and handed her to Heather. Heather calmed down when she realized that the baby was fine. She put Calandra back in the crib and we went into our room. The power was out from the storm. We laid down in bed and I gave Heather a kiss.

"Don't worry," I said, "everything is fine. Just get a good night sleep." We fell asleep.

"No," Heather screamed. She sat up straight and was breathing heavily. I sat up and looked at her. "Nightmare," she told me. "Don't worry about it." We laid back down and went back to sleep. Throughout the night we were awakened to Calandra crying, just as typical babies do.

The next morning Heather and I woke up and took Calandra downstairs. I was surprised to see that the storm didn't do that much damage. Just a few power lines and trees were down. The power was back on and the storm was gone. It was sunny out and it looked like it was going to be a nice day. I was still really agitated as to why we were having flashbacks all of a sudden. We never had flashbacks. People told me that we would have flashbacks right away but I guess we may have pushed them into our subconscious while on other missions. Now that we were on break, we had time to think about all of the things we experienced.

"So what's going on today," Heather asked.

"I think I'm going to call headquarters and make sure everything is alright," I replied. "I have a funny feeling."

"You worry too much," she continued, "take a break." She walked over and gave me a kiss.

"I'm the leader," I replied, "that's what I'm supposed to do."

"Yes, but your my husband, and a father," Heather responded, "you need to do that too."

"I know," I answered, "but I can't help worrying. I never left the team before."

"If they are your team, which they are, then trust them."

"I do. I just don't want them getting hurt."

"They're fine."

"Alright, but I need to call and make sure. Then I can relax." Heather laughed and took Calandra into the living room.

Meanwhile back in paradise, the others were trying to figure out how to get home.

"This is all William's fault," Chris replied.

"No," Steph butted in, "I won't let you blame it on him. You agreed to it."

"Not me," Krissy said. "I didn't want to go but you didn't give much of a choice."

"I agreed to ten minutes," Chris answered. "This is a bit more than ten minutes."

"It's not William's fault that the belts were destroyed," Steph continued.

"TJ will find a way to get us home," William said. "TJ won't let us down."

"TJ doesn't know," Krissy replied. "We didn't even get to tell him."

"He wouldn't have let us go," Chris answered.

"And for obvious reasons," Krissy commented. Chris stood up and started pacing back and forth.

CHAPTER NINE

In the present, Heather was watching Michael again. I was in the kitchen reading the newspaper. Heather was in the living room playing Candyland with Michael. Calandra was sleeping upstairs.

"Can I watch my dino movie," Michael asked.

"Not now," Heather said, "I don't like dinosaurs."

"I want to watch it now," Michael screamed!

"Alright," Heather replied, "you can watch it." Heather got up and put the movie in. "I'll be back in, when it gets to the dino attacks," Heather told Michael. She came out in the kitchen and looked to see what I was doing. She sat on the chair next to me. "Do you miss the missions," she asked me.

"No," I answered.

"Yes you do," she responded, "don't lie to me."

"Ok, I do," I replied, "but I love staying here with you and Calandra."

"Well then you won't mind if we quit the team," she continued.

"What," I asked, "you want to quit the team?"

"Yeah," she answered, "I figured that Calandra needs her parents and if we stay on the team, we could be killed." Just then Michael started screaming. Heather ran in and saw two dinosaurs fighting each other. There was a flash of light and she was back at the camp with the dinos watching us from the woods. Michael ran over and grabbed her leg in fear and she snapped out of it.

"I want to see the allosaurus," Michael told Heather. Heather shook her head yes. She took the remote and fast-forwarded the movie to the part where the allosaurus attacks the stegosaurus. The phone rang. Heather picked it up.

"Hello," Heather answered.

"Heather," the voice said, "this is Dr. Johnson. Is TJ there?"

"Yes," she replied, "hold on one moment." She took the phone away from her head and covered it with her hand. "TJ, telephone." I got up and walked in there. She handed me the phone.

"Hello," I answered.

"TJ, this is Dr. Johnson. Is the rest of the team there?"

"No, I answered. I thought they were with you."

"No, they're not. They were supposed to be traveling back to your place to get something that Steph forgot."

"Well we haven't seen them since they originally left. I don't know where they could be."

"Me either. They disappeared days ago."

"You know, I've had a weird feeling for awhile."

"Where could they be," Johnson asked. Just then the allosaurus roared on the movie. Suddenly I stopped and looked at the screen. My heart started beating fast and I was breathing more heavily. I took a big gulp. I knew where they were.

"I have to call you back." I hung up the phone.

"What was that about," Heather asked.

"He can't find the team," I replied.

"Where could they be," she asked.

"They are in the time of the dinosaurs," I answered. She laughed.

"You don't really think that do you."

"No I don't, I know that."

"Are you serious?"

"Yes, and they are stuck there. We need to help them. I'm calling my mom and dad to watch Calandra. We need to go back in time."

"You're crazy. You don't know that they are there. Plus the dinosaur period is such a wide range of years. You're talking about hundreds of millions of years."

"I know I can track them. I have to try." She just shook her head and thought about it.

"I'll call Michael's mom. Then I'll pack up." I smiled at her. I knew she couldn't say no. I dialed my mom and dad's number.

"Hello," my mom answered.

"Mom," I said, "can you watch Calandra?"

"Yeah sure," she said. "Why, is something wrong?"

"Great thanks," I yelled and hung up the phone. I ran upstairs and packed some clothes. We needed to head to D.C. to try and track them. Heather called Tasha and had her pick Michael up. I got Calandra ready as Heather packed her clothes. An hour later, we were ready to leave. We took Calandra to my parent's house.

"Mom," I said, "we need to go back in time. We'll be back as soon as possible. Thank you so much." We walked out and drove to D.C.

CHAPTER TEN

"Alright," Chris said, "as the leader, I say we need to build better shelters. I think that if we can build them on the edge of the high cliff, we will be safer."

"You don't know anything," Krissy replied. "Why should we listen to you?"

"Because," Chris answered, "I am the leader."

"He's right," Steph butted in, "we need to listen to him."

"Yeah," William added.

"But he didn't listen to TJ on the last mission," Krissy complained.

"Right," William agreed.

"Will you pick a side and stick to it," Steph told William.

"Yeah William," William said. "I mean, sure thing Steph."

"I didn't listen to TJ," Chris continued, "because he made some bad choices."

"Well maybe you are too," Krissy snapped back.

"Look," Chris screamed at her, "You don't want to agree with me, that's great! But I want you to stop arguing and let me move on with the rest of this team!"

"Whatever," Krissy replied unhappy about agreeing. "I will serve you mister dictator."

"What was that," Chris asked.

"You heard me," Krissy answered. Chris started walking upriver toward the cliffs. William and Steph followed. Krissy paused for a moment and then ran to catch up. On the way to the cliff Krissy kept an eye out. She didn't like Chris as the leader, she didn't trust his judgment. Actually, Krissy didn't like Chris at all. When they got to the top of the cliff, Chris stood looking off the edge.

"Now what, Mr. Leader," Krissy asked with sarcasm. "How do you suppose we get over to the other side?"

"Who says we want to," Chris asked back.

"Well there is no place to set up camp here," Krissy answered.

"Yes there is," Chris sharply replied, "right here!"

"Are you mad," Krissy continued. "Have you lost your mind? Did you go crazy during the walk? This is too easy for a predator to get us."

"You're the plump one," Chris snapped back, "they'll eat you first."

"I don't think this is a good place to camp," Steph added, "and I've never been here before."

"Well then," Chris said angrily, "why don't you find somewhere else to camp? I'll stay here." Just then they heard a roar. Chris turned toward the woods. Steph backed up. The ground was shaking and the trees in front of them were moving. Then the large dino from before came running out of the woods at them.. Krissy and Steph screamed. Chris grabbed Steph's arm and ran toward the woods to their left. William and Krissy followed. Chris climbed the first tree he felt was suitable. The others followed his lead up the tree.. The dino was approaching fast. Chris climbed to the top. The tree was right at the edge of the cliff. The giant dino ran into the tree and the tree fell over. The team grabbed onto a branch. They hung high over the river, about eighty feet up. Krissy looked down and screamed.

"Don't look down," Chris told her. The dino started pushing the tree off the cliff. Chris was debating what to do next. Jump or be eaten. "On three, let go of the branch," Chris screamed to the others. "One, two…" Before he could finish the dino had pushed the tree off the cliff and they were falling quickly toward the river. They all screamed as they hit the water. They went under and scurried to the surface. As they got to the surface they gasped for air. The tree landed near them. The current was taking them downstream. "Swim for shore," Chris yelled to the others. They started swimming toward the shore opposite the one that had the big dino on it. Chris climbed out and helped the others out. They sat down and caught their breath.

"Good idea, Chris," Krissy said still catching her breath, "next time, I'll ring the dinner bell for the dino." Chris just ignored the smart remark.

"So what's next," William asked, "where are we going to camp?"

"We climb this cliff and build shelters in one of the caves," Chris answered.

"Yeah," Krissy replied, "we'll be so much safer in the caves. After all they were only little dinos that attacked William and I."

"You have your choice," Chris continued, "little dinos or a big dino."

"One big one or hundreds of little ones," Krissy said. "Hmm, how do I choose? Which would kill me faster?"

"Me," Chris answered.

"Alright," Steph said, "this is not helping. We are stuck here and no matter what we do there is still the chance that we will be eaten, that's just the chance we have to take without choice."

"Yeah," William continued, "we can either keep fighting and die or be friends and die."

"I'll take the keep fighting and die choice," Chris answered. "At least I'll have fun the last minutes of my life, making fun of Krissy." They got up and started climbing up the cliff.

CHAPTER ELEVEN

"Now mister dictator," Krissy said, "are you happy that we are on this side of the river?"

"I don't know," Chris answered, "it depends if this side has one of those giant bad breath, smelly creatures. Oh, wait, there's one." He pointed to Krissy. "Brush your teeth."

"Would you suggest that I use my sock as a tooth brush," Krissy asked.

"Actually," Chris replied, "I think the dino next door has a brush you can borrow. Why don't you ask him?"

"Why don't you two knock it off," Steph commented.

"Yeah," William butted in, "knock it off."

"Stay out of this," Krissy and Chris replied sharply at the same time.

"Yeah," William continued, "stay out of it Steph." Steph looked at William and shook her fist. William took the opportunity to punch himself.

"Shut up, Chris," Krissy said, "or I'll slap the taste out of your mouth."

"Is that a threat," Chris asked.

"No, it was a threat," Krissy answered. Chris gave her a confused look. Krissy cracked him across the face and pushed him off the cliff. He fell and hit the water. Steph walked over to the edge and looked down. She turned to Krissy.

"You're in trouble now," Steph said. Before she could go on, she was on her way down to the river.

"What did you do that for," William asked.

"Do you want join them," Krissy replied.

"No sorry, love you," William quickly answered.

"Say that again and I won't think twice."

"I hate you."

"Say that again and I won't think once."

"I like you."

"How about shut up."

"Shut up." Krissy quickly threw William off the cliff. She wiped her hands. "That's just for your stupidity." Just then there was a roar in the background and Krissy ran off the cliff. Now that they were all in the river, again, they climbed to the shore that they were on the first time.

Back in Washington, Heather was in my office. "I agree that we need to save our team," Heather said, "but is it safe to try a new device? I mean remember what happened last time."

"I think it is fine," I replied, "Dr. Johnson wouldn't take another risk."

"But what if he didn't know it was a risk," she continued.

"That's a chance we have to take and I'm willing to take."

"I hate when you say that."

"Why?"

"Because nothing good has ever come out of that sentence."

"We faced this before, why not again?"

"Because last time we were young and stupid.

"So what are we now, old and stupid?"

"No, now we have Calandra to raise and we need to put her first. We can't just run off and have a good time without thinking about the risks."

"Who said this was going to be a good time? If we wanted to have a good time, there are safer ways."

"You know what I mean. See you don't listen to me. Either that or you don't care."

"I do care, but this is our job. We said that we would stick together as a team, no matter what."

"Well they are a team now, we are not part of it for six months."

"Actually, I told them to call me if they got a new mission

otherwise I would see them in six months. So they decided to take a new mission without us."

"Good, that leaves us to be safe, doesn't it?"

"Since then, I jumped through a window, you've been having massive nightmares, and Calandra almost had a shelf land on her. Does that sound like we are safe?"

"Safer than a huge predatory reptile chasing us at fifteen miles an hour, yeah."

"Well we can get shot, hit by a car, stabbed,…"

"Whatever, I get the picture, you don't listen to me anyway so we'll go."

"Good, then it's settled."

"See," Heather screamed as she ran out of the room and slammed the door.

"TJ and Heather please report to the lab," Johnson said over the intercom. I walked out of my office.

"Heather," I said, "come on."

"No," she replied, "you broke my trust. I trusted you on the past missions but now, you could care less about me or Calandra. Everyone was right, I should have left you. I didn't but I am quitting this team. End of story."

"Oh come on," I continued, "you know we can't do this without you. We said we are in or out as a team, that means you too. You agreed."

"That was when I didn't have a new-born daughter to worry about," she snapped back. "Life has priorities, you should think about it."

"TJ and Heather report to the lab immediately," Johnson said again over the intercom.

"I do have priorities," I said, "you and Calandra are first. But since neither of you are harmed, my team comes next. I don't understand why you changed your attitude all of a sudden."

"You must not know me," she continued, "I never liked our missions. I did them for you. You changed, not me. The last mission really showed the true you, didn't it?"

"The last mission, I put you first," I raised my voice, "that was the problem. Now I am doing the opposite and I am in the same situation. I can't win, can I?"

"You can't win," she replied, "when I am right." She started to walk away.

"Maybe, I should have reconsidered," I said, "I kept telling myself it wasn't a good idea to be involved with a team member. We were together in high school but maybe I should have ended the relationship when we joined the team. I guess I learned the hard way."

"TJ and Heather report to the lab, now!"

"So this was an experiment," Heather screamed in fury as she turned around. "That's all I am to you, an experiment!" She calmed down.

"This was a mistake, my mom was right. I should have avoided you. She told me all along that I was to involved. She said that we shouldn't have been that serious."

"So I'm a mistake," I replied, "and Calandra's a mistake."

"Yes," she said without thinking. I walked away. "No wait," she yelled to me, "that's not what I meant." She turned to the wall and kicked it. I walked down to the elevator and went in. I pressed the button to the basement. When I got down in the basement I walked into the lab.

"Where were you," Johnson asked with an impatient tone. "Where's Heather?"

"It's a long story," I answered "and Heather won't be going." He threw me my outfit and I took of my shirt and put on the blue shirt. Then I slipped off my pants and put the silver pants on. As I was getting dressed, he was explaining how the new belt works.

"It's like the old belts," he started, "you press the button. The only difference is that this time you will be shooting into the air, instead of down a black hole. You will fly into space and enter a black hole there. You will land basically the same way. This may be a little physically stressful."

"What do you mean, physically stressful," I asked.

"Well, it may cause damage to your body," he answered. He handed me the belt and I hooked it on. "It's just an experiment."

"Just like the first time," I said and smiled. He gave me a

backpack.

"In here is the suits for the others," he said. "It also has long shots, lasers, and other equipment. I put some food in there too, for the team, they probably haven't had a decent meal in a while." He handed me a pair of boots. I put them on. "These are special boots," he said, "they have some equipment built in them. They have booster packs to float but they need to be recharged every so often. And they have spikes to dig in, for climbing cliffs and other surfaces." I nodded to tell him that I understand. "The new communication equipment is on your belt." I nodded again. "This is it," he finished, "your rescue mission. Good luck." He shook my hand and I walked out of the lab. The backpack was extremely heavy. Probably because it had the boots and everything in it. It was huge. I took the elevator up to our offices.

"I have to leave," I told Heather. "I'm sorry for everything that has happened. I know I have been a real jerk at some points. But I want to clear this up, just in case I don't make it."

"What do you mean," she replied sadly. "Why wouldn't you make it?" She started to cry. She ran over and hugged me. "I'm sorry, too. I love you." Her hand slipped down my chest and hit the belt. Just then the wind picked up and our bodies started to shake. She looked at me in shock.

"Hold on," I said, "you hit the button." I programmed the belt to find the team's devices. We shot into the sky and Heather screamed. We went right through the roof, as if it wasn't there. We were flying through cold space. The pressure was painful. Heather was screaming in pain as we flew into the black hole. Once we entered the warp zone, the pressure stopped and we were fine. A few seconds later and we were standing in paradise. Heather looked around in awe. I knew we were in for a rude awakening, because rescue missions never go smoothly.

CHAPTER TWELVE

"Now we are back on the other side," Krissy said. "I wish we could just pick a side."

"I wish you would shut up," Chris replied. "I am trying to pick the best side."

"I wish there were bridges," William said. "It would be easier on me."

"How do you suppose we pick the best side," Krissy asked Chris.

"How about we'll stay on this side and you go on that side," Chris answered, "the one who survives is on the better side."

"Good idea," Krissy said as she started to walk away. Chris started to laugh. "Hey, that's not fair," Krissy whined when she caught on. Chris broke out laughing. They started to walk down the shore. They came upon some nests.

"What do you think it is," Steph asked. Just then they heard a sound in the woods. Chris stopped and looked around. He grabbed

Steph's shoulder and pushed her down in the vegetation. He laid down on the ground. Steph was laying next to him looking at him. Krissy and William did the same. A dino came walking over to one of the nests. It was about the size of a full grown human. It was rather skinny. It looked around, then it let out a cry. Chris saw the teeth. He knew immediately that it was a meat eater, but he had never seen this one before. Just then four more came running to the nests. They were green. William sneezed and they looked. William stood up and ran. They chased after him. The others stood up and more of the dinos appeared as if from out of nowhere. They surrounded the team. Chris grabbed an egg from the nest. The dinos cried out as they snapped at the team.

"Put it down," Krissy told Chris, "they are mad."

"They won't attack us as long as we have the egg," he replied. Just then one snapped at Steph and she stumbled backwards and fell on the nest. The dino ran over to her and slashed her arm. Then he snarled. She kicked it in the nose as it came down to sniff her. It picked its head up and shook it. She scurried up and ran. It chased after her. Krissy ran and two followed her. One came up from behind Chris and knocked him in the back with its head. He fell over and dropped the egg. It smashed on the ground. "Oh shit," Chris yelled in panic. He climbed to his feet and took off running. The rest followed him. He jumped in the river and swam to the other side. He met the others over there. The dinos were growling on the other side of the river. They couldn't cross.

"Well, we're back over here," Krissy said. She sat down in exhaustion. "I'm tired, I need to sleep."

"Alright," Chris said, "we'll take a nap. After all it is almost dark, we should just sleep to morning." They all agreed and they laid down.

Meanwhile, Heather and I were searching through the woods. Heather was having a problem pushing through the brush. I stopped and we sat down. I opened my backpack and handed Heather a bottle of water. Then I pulled out her suit, which Johnson put in even though she wasn't supposed to be going, and handed it to her. She got undressed and then put on the new outfit. She fixed her hair. I handed her the boots and she put them on. She took a sip of water and then handed it to me. I took a sip.

"We should just go home," she said, "this is pointless. I don't think we will find them."

"We have to try," I answered. She kissed me. A feeling of being watched came over me and I stopped and looked around. She looked at me, confused. She touched my face and kissed me again. I pulled away and looked around.

"What's wrong," she asked.

"We're being watched," I answered. She kissed me again. "Dinos," I continued. She jumped to her feet in fear. I stood up. Just then one of the dinos that had just attacked the team jumped in front of me. Heather screamed as it snapped at me. I punched it in the face. I pulled

165

out my laser and shot it at its eye. The dino screamed in pain and ran away. Heather ran over and put her arm around my waist. "I knew this stuff would come in handy," I said.

"Yeah," she replied, "it works better than any of the other Johnson experiments." I smiled at her. We started to walk again. We wanted to continue as long as we could before getting tired.

The next morning the others woke up. "We need to move on," Chris said. "We need to find a better place to camp."

"There is no better place to camp," Krissy replied. "As long as we are in this time period, we are not safe anywhere." Chris started walking away. They walked for a few hours and ended up in a field.

"This place looks familiar," Chris said.

"We were never here," Krissy replied, "I'll never forget this time period. I know we weren't here."

"I know," Chris continued, "but it looks way too familiar." He looked around trying to figure out where he was. Just then a little dino ran out into the field. He looked and suddenly he flashed back. He saw Heather and I walking in front of him. Then he knew he was here before. "I'm having a flashback," he continued, "I was here, with Heather and TJ. The dino ran into the field and then, and then what happened? I can't remember." Just then he heard screeching in his flashback. "Oh my God," he said in fear, "the flying creatures."

"What flying creatures," Krissy asked. "I don't remember any

166

flying creatures."

"That's because you weren't with us," Chris answered recalling the memory. "It was just Heather, TJ, and I. We were here, in this field, and we got attacked by flying creatures." He looked to the sky. "I threw a rock at the creatures as they dove for the dino and then they attacked us." Just then there was a screech from above. Chris looked back to the sky and saw the creature. He took a gulp and his breathing increased. More creatures joined the one above him. "Run!" They all ran as the creatures swooped down at them. One hit William to the ground. Another picked Chris up and then dropped him. One flew at Steph but she hit the ground and it missed her. Krissy avoided another by falling to the ground.

Meanwhile Heather and I were walking through the woods near the field. Just then we heard screaming. We started to run toward the screams. When we got to the clearing we saw the others being attacked by the creatures. "Let's go," I told Heather. She just shook her head and we ran into the field. The others were shocked to see us. I pulled out my laser and so did Heather. We shot it at the creatures and they screamed in pain as we hit them. They flew away. The others ran over.

"Nice of you to show up," Chris said.

"Yeah," Krissy continued, "as if you couldn't be here any sooner."

"Yeah," I said, "nice to see you too."

"Sorry," Krissy replied, "but we really need to get out of here."

"We could have been here sooner," I continued, "if we knew where you were."

"William and Steph wanted to see how the team started," Chris told us, "so we decided to take them back in time. We would have told you but you wouldn't have let us go."

"That's right," Heather replied, "for an obvious reason. Look where it got you."

"You two spent time together during the last mission," Krissy added, "look where that got you." Heather looked over at her with an evil eye.

"Don't start with that," Heather told her, "it has nothing to do with this situation. Plus I am happy with where I'm at. I would just rather be at home than in paradise."

"Oh," Krissy replied," that's a shame. I thought everyone dreamed of living in paradise."

"Not me," Heather said.

"Alright," I cut in, "Johnson gave us these new belts so we will be able to transport home. The problem is he only gave us two, I guess that is all he had."

"Just like Johnson to be unprepared," Chris said.

"It's just like you to take control," I mumbled.

"What was that," Chris asked.

"Nothing," I replied.

"No," Chris said, "you said I always take control. I'm not the one that chose to leave Steph behind."

"Did we," I asked. "If I remember that changed."

"Yeah because of me," he continued. "I stayed and saved her."
Steph looked at William.

"Don't bring this up," Steph cut in, "it has nothing to do with this mission."

"This isn't a mission," I said, "it's a game. A very dangerous game that should have been avoided." I looked at William and Steph. "Did you think this would be fun?"

"I just wanted to see it for ten minutes," William answered. "That's all I wanted."

"Our time traveling capabilities are for work only, not some fun thought up mission of yours."

"Alright," Chris yelled, "you can't totally take it out on him."

"Why," I asked. "Who should I take it out on?" There was a roar and a thud.

"Ok," Heather cut in, "let's worry about it at home where it's safe."

"Well if you hadn't shown up," Chris continued, "then we wouldn't have had to worry about it. But since you decided to save us, we have to listen to you yell at us." There was another roar and the ground was shaking.

"And I should," I continued. "I have a daughter at home to worry about and here I am in the middle of nightmare world. I told you if you had a mission call me, otherwise I'd see you in six months. In my book, taking a vacation to paradise, is not considered a mission."

"Who cares," Heather said, "we need to go now." There was another roar and the trees were moving.

"This wasn't a mission," Chris responded to me. "We just wanted to make William happy."

"If it wasn't a mission then you shouldn't have come," I told him.

"Who cares," Heather screamed now angry that we weren't leaving. "Now why don't you both stop arguing and start running because there is a t-rex coming from the woods!"

"That's not a rex," Chris replied, "that is an Allosaurus."

"Whatever," Heather continued to scream. "If it's going to eat us I want to get out of here." William, Krissy, Steph, and Heather started to run. Heather noticed that Chris and I were just standing there so she came back. We were staring into the woods.

"What is it," Heather asked me.

"Th-th-the Allosaurus isn't what we should be afraid of," I mumbled.

"Then what do you suggest we be afraid of," she asked in confusion.

"The raptors that are standing in the woods over there," I continued.

"Those are not raptors," Chris said. "Man you people watch too much Jurassic Park."

"Who cares what it is," I yelled. Just then I heard a loud screech come from the air. I looked up and saw that the pteros were back. "Oh great," I said, "we are in a lot of trouble."

CHAPTER THIRTEEN

There were four raptor-like dinos watching us from the woods, an allosaurus searching the perimeter, and pteros above us.

"Heather," I said, "you take Krissy and William with you and I'll take Chris and Steph." Heather nodded in agreement. "Let's get out of this nightmare once and for all. On three, one, two, three." We programmed the belts and pressed the warping buttons on our belts. We shot up into space. Chris and Steph were holding on tight to me. Krissy and William were squeezing Heather so much that she could hardly breathe. We landed in a field in the dark of night. Above us were the stars. All around was open field. I started to walk around.

"Where are we," Heather asked.

"I don't know," I replied. "We should be in our headquarters, but we're not." I took the flashlight from my belt and started searching for clues.

"Why aren't we in D.C.," Chris asked. "Was there a

malfunction?"

"I don't know," I snapped at him. "We must be in the present." Heather walked over to me and pulled out her flashlight. She grabbed onto my arm. She knew where we were.

"TJ," she said quietly and in fear, "tell me we're not where I think we are. Please tell me that." I continued to look around. I couldn't answer her question, I didn't know for sure.

"Where are we," Krissy demanded to know.

"You want to know," I screamed. "You are all so curious that you can't let me find out for sure." They backed off in shock. "I'll show you where we are." I took the flashlight and shined it into the woods then I started screaming.

"TJ," Heather said, "you're scaring me, stop!"

"What is he doing," Steph asked Chris.

"He's gone crazy," William added. Just then there was a loud roar from the woods. The others turned in shock. They realized we were back in paradise, just like Heather and I realized minutes ago.

"Oh my God," Heather said in fear with her face turning pale, "it's happening all over again." She started breathing real heavy and the temperature was cold enough that we could see her breath. Her eyes filled up with water and she dropped to her knees crying.

"What is she talking about," William asked.

"Our first mission," Chris replied. "It's happening again." I walked over and picked Heather off the ground.

"Stop it," I told her. "This doesn't help." She continued to cry. I let go of her and she fell to the ground again. I walked away.

"Now what do we do," Steph asked Chris.

"I don't know," he replied.

"We could always use this," Krissy said. She pulled her cell phone from her back pocket. I looked over to her.

"You had a cell phone all this time and you just tell me now," Chris responded. "You idiot! We could have solved this problem right away." Chris took the cell phone and started dialing. I walked over and grabbed the cell phone. I threw it against a rock and it shattered into pieces.

"That's it," I screamed in fury. "I make the calls from here on out. I'm the leader, I make the decisions, and a cell phone won't work 65 million years before they were invented."

"For your information," Chris replied, "it was ringing."

"Oh just great," Krissy said, "you broke my cell phone. Now we can't call for pizza and I'm starving."

"We can use mine," Steph said, "if you want to call."

"I'll call," Krissy said. Steph gave her the phone. Krissy walked away from the group and dialed.

"Now Johnson will know to send a team to rescue us," Chris said.

"Hey guys," Krissy yelled from where she was standing. "What's our address?"

"Just tell Johnson to send a team to the time of the dinosaurs," I told her.

"Johnson," Krissy said in confusion, "I thought you wanted me to order pizza. I'm on the phone with Pizza Please, not Johnson." I ran over and grabbed the phone and hung up. I dialed Johnson's number. His answer machine picked up.

"This is Dr. Johnson," the machine recited as it was fading out, "I am not in right now. Please leave a message and I'll get back to you as soon as possible." The machine beeped and then the phone shut off. I looked at the screen and it was blank. I threw it against the rock.

"Hey," Steph said, "what are you doing?"

"It had a dead battery," I told her.

"I have another battery," she replied.

"Does anyone have another cell phone," Chris asked. Everyone shook their head no. Heather was laying silently on the ground. I ran over to check on her. She was sleeping. I pushed on her shoulder to wake her up. She wouldn't wake up. I kept pushing on her shoulder because I wanted to see if she brought her cell phone.

"This is your fault," Chris told me, "you made her upset. She went into denial and shut down."

"Shut up," I said, "she's just tired."

"If that was the case she would wake up," Chris continued. "You have been so nasty and self-centered lately."

"Well it must be when I'm around you," I responded. "Because when we weren't on the team, I didn't fight with her."

"Then maybe you should quit the team," Chris thought he solved the problem.

"No," Steph, Krissy, and William chimed in together.

"They can't quit the team," Steph said, "he is a great leader. Plus we said 'all for one and one for all.'"

"What," Chris responded, "are we the three Musketeers?" I pushed on Heather's shoulder again. She still wouldn't move.

"What is wrong with her," I screamed. "Why isn't she waking up?" Just then William fell over. Steph and Chris ran over to check on him.

"He won't wake up either," Steph told me.

"What is going on," Krissy asked in panic. I took my flashlight and looked for any clue as to why they were falling asleep and not waking up. Just then Krissy fell over.

"What is going on," Steph asked.

"I don't know but we have to get out of here," I told them, "and we need to go now."

"Right," Chris added, "we need to go now." Then he fell over. I looked at Steph in fear.

"Get down," I told Steph. "Pretend your sleeping." We both laid down and stayed very still. A few minutes later a dinosaur ran out from the woods. It was about five feet high, very skinny, green in color, and had a very weird mouth. I had never seen this one before. The dino let out a cry and a few more ran into the field from the woods. The other members started to wake up and so we all stood up. Just then the dinos cried out and released some kind of purple gaseous chemical from their mouths. The chemical got to William and he fell over again.

"That's what it is," I said. "Chris grab William and run." Chris picked up William and we all started running. The dinos chased us. I was trying to figure what we could do to get away from them. "Run for the river," I yelled to the others. We started through the woods toward the river. When we got to the river we jumped in. William woke up when water splashed in his face. The dinos were nowhere in sight.

"Coast is clear," Heather said.

"Let's head to camp," I said, "and begin our first mission all over again." Heather gave me a weird look.

CHAPTER FOURTEEN

"Do you think Calandra's ok," Heather asked me. We were laying in our tent. She had her head on my chest and her arms wrapped around my waist.

"She's fine," I told her. "She's with my mom and dad."

"I know," she said, "but I still have this feeling about the follower of the Master of Time."

"Don't worry about it."

"I know I shouldn't but he did bomb our headquarters." I held her closer.

"She's fine. My mom and dad won't let anything happen to her." I gave her a kiss.

"But the enemy is more experienced," Heather continued. "He's going to attack us where it hurts most. Your mom and dad won't know enough about how to defend her."

"Sure they will," I told her, "it's a natural instinct for parents and grandparents to protect their children and grandchildren."

"Alright, I give up. She's fine. You're right, as always." I gave her a kiss and we went to bed.

I was standing in front of an altar. In the altar were four coins, one for earth, fire, wind and water. It was the Temple of the Elements. I had always believed it to be a myth but now, here they were straight in front of me. The creators of the world as we know it, the Elements. Then I saw it, the last of the five elements. Karma, which made life and determined destiny. I began to fly down a deep dark tunnel toward pure darkness. All that could be heard was a baby crying and it sounded like Calandra. Then the team was defeated and the world overturned by the Elements. Each team member died in a different way. Chris was burned to death, William was thrown off a cliff, Steph was drowned, and Krissy was left to be killed by a tornado. I, on the other hand, was killed by Karma.

"That's what happened in my dream," Heather told me. She was woken up by some nightmare and she startled me with her scream.

"What do you think it means," I asked her.

"I don't know," she said, "but it doesn't look good."

"What would Calandra have to do with it," I asked. "What would the Elements want with a young baby?"

"I can't answer that. I wish I could though. I am really worried about Calandra." Just then I heard some growling outside the tents. I got up and ran out. It was a pack of the dinos snarling at Krissy. They looked at Heather and I when we got outside.

"Krissy," I yelled, "don't just sit there. Run!" Krissy took off toward the river. She jumped in as dinos followed her. They wouldn't jump in so they turned their attention to Heather and I. "Go," I told Heather, "jump in the river."

"I won't leave you," she replied.

"You have to," I continued. "What about Calandra?" Heather took off for the river and a bunch followed her. She jumped in. I yelled at the dinos to distract them. They came running towards me. I took off into the woods because I knew that if I jumped in the water that they might follow. I was pushing branches out of my face as I ran. They were catching up very quickly. I jumped up at one of the branches on the tree nearby. I swung myself up onto the branch and quickly continued the rest of the way up the tree. They jumped up and snapped at my feet. I wasn't out of the clear. Just as I jumped up to the next branch they snatched the one from underneath me. Finally I got out of reach and I sat catching my breath. When they were gone, I slowly climbed back down. I started to walk back to camp when I heard some rustling in the woods. I stopped and looked around. Then I saw the dinos. They were hunting other dinosaurs, but now they saw me. They jumped out from where they were hiding and I started running the other direction. They continued to chase me. I was swerving through the woods hoping to lose them. They were falling behind because of the branches hitting them. Just then I tripped over a branch and fell flat on my face. I couldn't move. Then I saw darkness.

"I have to help TJ," Chris told the others. "William come with me." William and Chris started running through the woods. Heather sat down on the rock and started to pray. Chris was pushing through the trees and bushes. William, on the other hand, was having a bit more of a problem.

The dinos continued to snap at me as I came back to consciousness. I still couldn't move. I couldn't tell if I was paralyzed or not but I couldn't move. They were screeching and yapping at each other. Probably deciding who got to eat first. Just then Chris and William ran in and kicked them in the mouth.

"Run," Chris yelled to William. "Get them away from TJ." They started running toward the field. All the dinos followed them. Now that I had time to see why I couldn't move I saw that I was tangled in some bushes. I fought to free myself. When I was free, I grabbed a huge branch and started running as fast as I could toward the field. I couldn't run very fast because I hurt my ankle during the fall. When I got to the field I saw that the dinos were gone but that William and Chris were being attacked by pteros. One grabbed William by the shirt and took him up into the air. Then it let go of him and he hit the ground with a thud. He got up and started running again. I ran out into the field. A ptero swooped down at me and grabbed me by the shoulders and I lost the branch. Its claws dug into my shoulder and I screamed in pain. I tried to wiggle myself free as it took me higher and higher into the sky. It dropped me and I fell screaming all the way down to the ground. I laid there motionless and in pain. Chris ran immediately toward me. A ptero swooped down and knocked him over as it tried to grab a hold of him but missed. William ran for the cliffs that were on the other side of the field.

"No," Chris screamed to William, "those are their cliffs. Don't run to them." William stopped dead in his tracks. As he did a ptero swooped down and grabbed him. It took him up and dropped him off at one of the cliff ledges. He screamed for help.

"Hold on," I yelled to him as I climbed to my feet. I started to run toward the cliffs, limping. A ptero swooped down and knocked me over. I fell on my back and as it came back around I kicked it and it flew backwards and hit the ground. I climbed as quickly as I could to my feet and started running toward the cliffs again. I started climbing the cliffs as fast as I could. A bunch of pteros started to peck at William.

"Jump," Chris yelled to him.

"No," I told them, "he'll never survive the fall."

"He'll never make it up there either," Chris responded. William jumped, falling all the way to the ground. He rolled as he hit the ground and laid there motionless. I bowed my head and then I saw Chris do the same. I let go of the cliff and fell to the ground. When I got back up to my feet, I noticed something extraordinary. William moved, he was alive.

He actually survived the fall.

"Watch out," I screamed to Chris as a ptero swooped down from behind him. He ducked but the ptero still grabbed him. He wiggled free and just as the ptero was going to grab him again, one of the dinos that chased me snatched the ptero in its jaws. More of the dinos ran into the field and the pteros flew up to their ledges.

"Let's get out of here," Chris said, "while we still can." We walked quickly and quietly toward the woods. The dinos saw us walking though so they started to chase us.

"Run," I screamed! We started running through the woods toward the camp. Once again pushing the branches out of our way. The dinos caught up to us quickly. There was a stream in front of us. I grabbed onto one of the branches above us and swung over the stream to the other side. Chris and William did the same. The dinos wouldn't cross the stream.

"We're clear," Chris said. "They won't come across." Just then there was a loud roar.

"You shouldn't have spoken so soon," I told Chris. We ran quickly toward camp.

CHAPTER FIFTEEN

When we got back to camp the girls were gone. "Where could they have gone," William asked. "They should have stayed here."

"What they should have done and what they did are two different things," I responded.

"Yeah" Chris continued, "they probably went looking for us."

"Well," I said, "we need to go looking for them." We heard a loud roar and knew what was happening. We started running through the woods again. This time we weren't being chased but instead needed to help the girls before they were killed. We tried to follow the roars and the screams. It sounded like it was coming from all directions.

"Where are they," William cried in fear.

"I don't know," Chris said in panic.

"Keep searching," I told them trying to stay calm. "And keep your ears and eyes open." Just then I heard a loud scream. "That way!" I pointed and we started running.

"Down here," Heather yelled. I looked and saw an underground cave opening. It was straight down. They must have fell down.

"Are you ok," I yelled back to her.

"We're fine," she answered, "just get us out of here quick. And watch for the…" Just then there was a loud roar from behind us. "Allosaurus," she continued. I turned around and saw the allosaurus standing there.

"You two have to distract the dino," I told them. "I have to try to get them out of the cave.

"Right," Chris responded. He started yelling and the allosaurus looked. Then William and Chris took off running and the dino chased them. I started immediately to try to get them out. I took a some plants and started tying them together. Then I slid them down into the cave.

"I got it," Heather said.

"Just be careful climbing up," I told her. "I don't know how safe this is." She tugged on it and the started climbing up it. Just then there was a bright flash and a boom of thunder.

"Just great," Krissy screamed, "a thunderstorm." Heather climbed out and then Krissy started up next.

"Hurry," Steph told Krissy, "I want to make it out of here too." Heather grabbed onto me in fear. She knew as well as I did that this was worse than the first time we were here. Just then, as Krissy was climbing out of the cave, a lightning bolt struck nearby and started the trees on fire. Krissy fell in fear and she hit the cave floor.

"Is she alright," I yelled down to Steph.

"I'm fine," Krissy yelped back in pain.

"Hurry Krissy," Heather screamed to her, "the forest is on fire." Steph started climbing up so that Krissy could regain her strength. Heather was covering her face in fear. The fire was spreading quickly. It started to rain but not enough to put the fire out. The wind was picking up.

"Hurry," I yelled to them, "this storm is intensifying fast." I pulled Steph out as she reached the top. "Go," I told Heather and Steph, "run for camp."

"No," Heather demanded, "I won't split from the group."

"Yeah," Steph continued, "all for one and one for all." I shook my head. There was a loud roar and a thud.

"Go now," I told them. They looked at each other and agreed that they were going to wait here. Krissy was climbing slowly up the rope-like object I created.

"Hurry," Heather screamed in fear, "the fire is near, the smoke is thick, the storm is intense, and there is a dino heading this way." Krissy tried to speed it up a little more but she was in too much pain to move fast. The trees were really swaying in the wind now. The smoke started to blow our direction and we started to cough. Krissy reached the top and I pulled her out. Heather fell over from the smoke. I picked Heather up.

"Run," I told Steph and Krissy. We started running in the direction of camp. Then in front of us, an allosaurus popped out. "Turn!" We turned left and started running as fast as we could. "Head for the river!" We ran for the river as quick as we could but the allosaurus was still after us. A bolt of lightning struck down behind us and cut the dino off. We were safe from the allosaurus for now. We kept running for the river.

"We can't jump in the river in the middle of a thunderstorm," Steph complained. "That's just plain stupid." We made it to the river and we walked to camp.

When we got to camp, I put Heather in our tent. The wind had died down and the storm was weak. It was just raining. Chris and William were still not there. I looked to the east and saw that the sun was rising. We all sat down to catch our breath. Heather woke up and came out to sit by us.

"This is much worse than our first trip," Heather commented.

"You're telling me," Krissy said. "This is crazy."

"This is more of a nightmare than before," I told them. "This is the worst place in time."

"I hope we can get out of this place soon," Heather said.

"Don't count on it," I told her, "the chances are just not there."

"Thanks for all the hope," Krissy responded. "I really feel better now."

"There is no sense in having false hope," I told Krissy.

"TJ is right," Steph added. "We need to face the facts.

CHAPTER SIXTEEN

Meanwhile back in the present, some criminal activity was taking place. The problem was in the Master of Time's headquarters. "We need to get the team while they are gone," the new leader told the thugs. "Here's our chance to snag the kid and hit the leaders where it hurts most. That's the only way to weaken them." He laughed evilly.

Meanwhile, in Johnson's office, Johnson was sitting at his desk working on some paper work. The phone rang and he picked it up. "Dr. Johnson," he answered. "How can I help you?"

"Dr. Johnson," the person on the other line said. "This is Betty, TJ's mom."

"Oh, how are you," Johnson asked.

"Concerned," my mom continued. "Why haven't they returned yet?"

"Who," Johnson asked. "Why hasn't who returned?"

"The team," my mom answered. "They never returned."

"Oh," Johnson said in confusion, "I totally forgot they went into the past."

"How could you forget?"

"I have been so busy that I forgot that they were gone. I am so stupid sometimes." My mom just sighed.

"Just tell me why they haven't returned."

"Honestly, I don't know. I'll check into it though."

"Thank you, I'm watching Calandra and I am getting worried about them."

"No problem, just doing my job." He hung the phone up. He rubbed his face because he was really stressed out. "Ok," he said to himself, "check on the team. Check on the team." He saw a newspaper sitting on his desk.

The newspaper read, "Yankees Won the Game Last Night."

"Right," he told himself, "the team is winning. But why would Betty want me to check on the Yankees? Oh, duh, she wanted me to check on the Warriors." He looked at the newspaper.

"Golden State Warriors Lost Another Game," the newspaper read.

"Right," he said, "they lost. That still doesn't make sense though. Why wouldn't she just use her newspaper? Oh, duh, the Time Warriors. The Time Warriors! Yikes!" He ran out of his office and down the hall. He walked up to the secretary.

"Can I help you, Johnson," the secretary asked.

"Did I get any calls from the Time Warriors," he wanted to know.

"Let me check," she answered. She looked at the phone log. "No sir," she continued, "it doesn't look that way." He nodded his head and walked back to his office. He sat down and rubbed his head.

"Why wouldn't they come home," he said to himself. "I got it," he yelled. "I'll check my phone history." He picked up his phone and dialed a number. The computer from the phone company started to read off numbers that had called.

"555-2114, 555-1245, 555-1787, 555-1918…," the computer read.

"That's it," he said, "555-1918 is the number for Steph's cell phone. They did call. Ok, computer, process when the number 555-1918 called please." It was a few minutes before he got a response.

"Yesterday," the computer responded, "but the location is unclear."

"Thank you," he said as he hung up the phone. "They need help and they're going to get it." He ran quickly out of his office and down the hall.

CHAPTER SEVENTEEN

Chris and William returned and we were all sitting around talking. There was not much more that we could do. There was a rumble and some roars. The trees around us started swaying and then the earth began to crack.

"Earthquake," Steph screamed.

"Stay calm," I instructed. The ground was splitting all around us. Then it split Heather and I from the rest of the group. "You four try to stay together," I told them. Heather grabbed onto my arm. We were close to the river and they were close to the woods. Just then the allosaurus burst out from the trees. The four of them took off running. "In the river," I told Heather, "and swim across." We jumped in the river and started across. When we got to the other side we started to climb up the cliff.

The others were running through the woods with the allosaurus chasing them. Trees were falling all around them from the Earthquake. They were having a hard time staying on their feet. "Keep running," Chris yelled, "no matter what." They were running around the small cracks. The dino was roaring. It was really mad at something. "Climb the tree," Chris told them. They started to climb the tree and when they got to safety they sat catching their breath.

Meanwhile we got to the top of the cliff. Heather and I stood looking around thinking how we could meet back up with the group. Just then we heard a cry from behind us. We turned around to see a dino standing there. It looked really mad, I think we were in its territory. I had no idea what it was but I could see its teeth. It cried out and ran at us.

The dino ran at us and we moved out of the way. We started running toward the woods. The dino chased after us. We climbed the first tree we got to.

"It's just defending its territory," Heather told me. The dino ran into the tree and Heather fell off the branch but I grabbed her and pulled her up. The dino ran into the tree again. Finally, it left and we sat there waiting to make sure that the coast was really clear.

The other members were still sitting in the tree when they heard a cry from above. This time they looked up and it was a creature bigger than the other flying creature.. It was two times bigger. It was screeching and more joined it. They sat there admiring this giant flying creature.

"Do you think it will hurt us," Krissy asked.

"It doesn't look friendly," Steph answered. They climbed down before it attacked the tree. William took off running through the woods toward the field.

"Where is he going," Chris asked. "If he goes into the field it will get him easier."

"That's where he is heading," Krissy responded. "We better hurry." They took off chasing William and the flying creature followed from above. William ran out into the field and the creature swooped down and knocked him over. He got up and started to run again. The creature flew high into the sky and then swooped down again. The other three members ran into the field and screamed to William.

"Run for the woods," Chris yelled to him but William was ignoring it.

"Why won't he listen," Krissy asked.

"Because he wants to make our journey more exciting than it already is," Steph answered. "That's what William does." The creature picked him up and then dropped him.

"It's going to be real exciting," Chris added, "when he is dead." William continued to run through the field and the creature chased after him screeching the whole way.

"You have to help him," Krissy told Chris.

"What do you want me to do," Chris asked. "I can't just kill Big Bird, it wouldn't be right."

"But Big Bird is going to kill William," Krissy continued. "You have to do something."

"Do you have a weapon," Chris asked Krissy.

"No," Krissy responded. "Why?"

"Well what do you suggest I kill it with," Chris demanded to know.

"I don't know," Krissy replied, "just do something already!" Chris shook his head.

"I must be stupid or crazy. One of the two," he said as he started to run into the field. The creature picked William up and dropped him. Chris ran over and knocked William over right as the creature was going to pick him up again. The creature missed which just made it even more mad. It screamed in fury as it flew back up into the sky. Chris knew he was in a lot of trouble again. He grabbed William by the arm and started pulling him toward the woods. William tried to get loose. The creature flew back down. Krissy and Steph covered their eyes as it flew past them. It grabbed both Chris and William at once. It flew into the sky. Chris started to wiggle free. He fell to the ground. William did the same but the creature caught him as he fell. Chris followed it from the ground. William was now screaming as it was heading for the cliffs.

"Try to wiggle free," Chris told William. William did exactly that. It wasn't working though. The creature dropped him at one of the ledges on the side of the cliff. There were many more creature nests around him, maybe even hundreds. The creature headed back to the field to go after Krissy and Steph. They ran into the woods. Chris climbed up the side of the cliff but not easily though. There were flying reptiles all over the place. He climbed from ledge to ledge and jumped wherever he could. The creatures chased him and knocked him over. He got back up and continued running toward William. When he got to the ledge that William was standing on, he grabbed William by the arm and led him from ledge to ledge away from the nests. When they got to a low enough ledge, they jumped. They hit the ground and rolled. The creatures swooped down and they climbed quickly to their feet and started to run again.

"Hurry," Steph screamed from the woods. They ran across the field as fast as they could as the creatures, about ten to fifteen of them, chased from above. They got close to the edge of the woods right as the creatures were about to swoop down and grab a hold of them. William and Chris dove for the trees and the creatures missed. They climbed to their feet and started running through the woods with Krissy and Steph following.

Four of the raptor-like dinos were waiting for them in the woods and they took off after the group. The group was running for their lives. The dinos followed in close pursuit. Again the only thing that kept the dinos from getting the group were the branches that were hitting them as they ran. They were running for the river. Just then four more dinos jumped out in front of them and four from each side. They were completely surrounded.

"Oh great," Krissy said, "we're dead." Steph was breathing really heavy.

"Not very good odds," Chris added. "Sixteen dinos to the four of us."

"Hey," I yelled, "over here." The dinos turned and saw Heather and I standing there waving our arms. They decided to chase after us. All sixteen of them took off after us. We ran for the field. When we got to the field the dinos ran out after us. Heather and I turned quickly and they slid past us. They screeched as they tried to get back on the path behind us. The flying reptiles were flying over head. Just then there was a loud roar from the woods nearby. Heather and I stopped dead in our tracks. The dinos ran over and jumped at us but before they could reach us, a plant-eater got in their way and they attacked that instead. Heather and I sighed in relief and started walking back toward the other members.

CHAPTER EIGHTEEN

Meanwhile, back in the present, my parents were sitting watching television. Calandra was upstairs sleeping in the crib that I used when I was a baby. "Turn on the news," my dad told my mom. "Maybe they can tell us something about the team."

"I don't really like the news," my mom replied. "It's too depressing."

"I know but it's the only way we'll find out about the team," my dad continued. My mom decided to put CNN on. They were covering sports at the time. They both got up and walked out of the room and into the kitchen to get something to drink.

"Breaking news," the newsperson said, "this just in." My mom and dad knew it had to be something to do with us so they ran into the room quickly. "The Master of Time has a group of followers still surviving and the government believes that they are going to attack the team. The government has reason to believe that there is someone in charge that is being covered by people like the Master of Time. If you remember last time, the group barely beat the Master of Time and his allies. Anyone who knows the team is encouraged to keep an eye open." Just then there was a bang coming from upstairs.

"The baby," my mom screamed. My mom and dad ran upstairs quickly. They found a few guys standing near the baby.

"We're taking the kid," the one said.

"Not if we can help it," my dad responded.

"What are you doing," my mom asked my dad. "Are you crazy? They'll kill you."

"I have to defend Calandra," he answered with bravery. My mom ran out of the room and dialed for the police. The thugs threw the lamp that was nearby at my dad and he ducked. One of the thugs grabbed Calandra from the crib and took off out the window and down the street. The other thugs followed. My dad ran down the steps and out the door after them. My mom was standing at the door watching. The thugs were running as fast as they could down the street toward their car. They parked far away so they wouldn't make too much noise sneaking up on the house. They hopped in the car and started to drive away but were cut off by the police in the front. They put the car in reverse, but more police came from behind. Then from the ally streets on the sides of them. They were surrounded. The police took care of the thugs and returned the baby to my mom and dad. My mom sighed with relief.

In Washington D.C., Johnson was preparing one of our old devices to help us. He was connecting wires quickly and putting the machine together. "If I send this into time," he said, "they can use it to come home."

CHAPTER NINETEEN

The next morning when we woke up, I gathered up some fruit for breakfast. The sky was a weird color today. "Why is the sky that color," Chris asked. It was almost like a gray and green mixed together.

"I think it means an intense storm is on the way," I answered. "That would be my guess."

"Great," Heather added, "like we didn't have enough problems." .

"Do you want to go for a walk," I asked Heather. She nodded her head "yes." We walked up to the waterfall and just stood there. There, the sky was bright blue, so I knew the storm was coming from the other direction. The mist from the waterfall was so strong today that it was lightly covering us. On the other side of the canyon, there were some brachiosaurs. Brachiosaurs are large dinosaurs, that stand on all fours, with long necks for reaching the leaves on top of trees. The sun was shining brightly down on the waterfall and creating a really cool glare. I looked into the waterfall and saw an opening behind it.

"What's that," Heather asked as she realized what I was looking at.

"I don't know," I answered, "but we're going to find out."

"Just great," she said, "more exploring." We started to climb down the canyon cliff. We walked along the edge of the river toward the waterfall. When we got to the waterfall we ran behind it getting soaked. Heather was laughing and the water was warm. We walked into the opening and inside it looked almost like a cave. We walked through the tunnel; the amount of light was decreasing. I took my flashlight out and started shining it around and then Heather did the same. The sight was awesome, there were crystals hanging all around us. They sparkled in the light of our flashlights.

"Wow," Heather said, "this is awesome." I was trying to figure out what it was. Then I realized that the temperature was much colder in the cave than outside.

"It's not crystals," I told Heather, "it's ice."

"But what would cause it," she asked.

"The water underground is cooling down quickly," I told her. "Environmental change is taking place." We stood there marveling at the sight. Then there was a roar from deep inside the cave.

"Let's go," Heather said, "I don't think I want to meet up with the occupant."

"Right," I responded, "just give me a second."

"No, let's go now," she continued. "That didn't sound good."

"I want to know what it is," I told her.

"I don't," she cried. "I know it wants us for breakfast." It roared again just louder, and then there were other roars. Next came some really loud stomping sounds.

"Ok," I told her, "time to go." We started running toward the entrance of the tunnel. Then behind us came a giant dinosaur. It had a huge, elongated neck. The dinosaur opened its mouth and roared. It had sharp teeth indicating it was a meat-eater.

"Oh my God," Heather screamed. We got to the entrance of the cave.

"Jump in the water," I told her as we ran to the sides of the canyon, "it won't come in after us." We jumped in and the dino followed us into the water.

"It won't follow us into the water huh," Heather cried in panic. "What do you call this?"

"I call this swim for the sides and climb the canyon," I answered in as much fear as her. We did exactly that and as we were climbing the canyon, the dino was snapping at us. When we got to the top we stopped to rest. Just then there was some heavy breathing behind us and a roar. We turned around to see dinosaur standing there. "Holy shit," I cried in fear. We started to run down the sides of the canyon as it chased us.

"That's an allosaurus," Heather told me as we ran.

"I know that," I replied.

"Alright," I told Heather, "we should be far enough away from the big dino that we can jump in the river." I grabbed her hand and we jumped off the canyon once more. We fell to the river and fought to the surface.

"I hope that's the last time we ever have to do that," Heather said. I was hoping the same but I had a lot of doubt in my mind. Something told me that we would be doing that again. Something told me that we would return to 'paradise' again. We swam to the side of the river and walked back to camp. When we got back to camp the storm was really intense. The trees were swaying and there were loud cracks of thunder in the distance. The sky was a really dark green now.

"That's a sign of a tornado," Krissy told me.

"I know," I responded, "and that is not a good thing."

"No kidding," Chris said.

"Let's get out of here," William told us.

"Where should we go," I asked him.

"Let's find a cave," Steph said, "and wait the storm out."

"From our previous experience," Heather replied, "we don't want to wait the storm out in a cave." It started pouring. The wind was really strong now. We were having a hard time hearing each other as we spoke.

"We need to do something," Heather cried to me. "You're the leader make a decision."

"What do you want me to do," I asked her. "I have no alternatives.

It's just too dangerous." Just then there was a sound of a loud freight train. I looked and saw a tornado moving toward us. "Here's my decision, run!" We started running for the field. I knew that if we stayed in the woods we wouldn't find shelter from the tornado. The lightning was right above us now. It was striking nearby trees. The tornado was destroying everything in its path. Then a lightning bolt struck some trees in front of us and started the woods on fire.

When we made it into the field the woods all around us were on fire. Just then I heard a screech from above. There were more flying creatures flying in circles above us. One swooped down and grabbed Heather. I grabbed onto Heather's legs as it lifted her into the sky. She looked down at me and screamed. It took us really high into the sky.

"Let me climb up you," I told her. "I can hit it." I started to climb up over her. The creature dug its claws into her shoulder and she screamed in pain. I climbed up onto the creature's back and punched it in the head. It started to descend and I hit it again. We were getting closer and closer to the ground.

"Watch out," Chris yelled to me. I looked and saw another creature flying toward me. It knocked me over on the back of the one I was on. I stood up and it came down again. I grabbed on to its legs and it took me up. Then it flew back toward the other and I kicked the one that had Heather as we flew by it. It released Heather and she fell to the ground. I tried to wiggle myself free but it didn't work. Just then there was a flash of light and a time belt appeared in my hand.

"Thank you Johnson," I said to myself. I knew I had to hit the button. If I did the creature would be startled and drop me. I would have to protect the belt as I fell and then grab a hold of the team before I got taken into the warp zone. It was risky but it was the only option I had.

"Do it," Heather yelled to me. "What else can you do?" I nodded my head and hit the button. The wind picked up and the creature dropped me in fear. I tucked the belt closely into myself and hit the ground. I jumped to my feet and grabbed a hold of the team. The ground disintegrated around us and turned into a black hole. It was our old device, that I liked so much more. Then we fell into the warp zone and flew through the tunnel toward the light. We shot out into space.

"I hope this works," Krissy screamed.

"I do too," I responded. The earth started to turn clockwise. When it stopped we fell to the surface. It was dark and we were in the middle of a field again.

"Not again," Heather cried, "you have to be kidding me." We all looked around, breathing heavily, hoping to find out that we were in the present. Then, when I looked to my left, I saw the city of Washington D.C. and I tapped the others on the shoulder and pointed. We all sighed in relief.

"We're home," William cried in relief.

"Now I know how your team started," Steph said in exhaustion.

"Never, ever again," Krissy told them. "And I mean NEVER!"

"I agree," Chris replied to Krissy. "But you should never say NEVER!"

"It's over," Heather said as she smiled, "it's finally over."

"For now," I responded.

MISSION SIX:

THE ELEMENTS

CHAPTER ONE

3 Years Later. Unknown Location

"**H**ow do I beat the team," the man asked the psychic. He was there hoping to find the answers. The woman was supposed to be the best psychic in the world.

"The Master of Time tried," she responded, "but he failed, foolishly. If you want to beat the team, you must first get me the treasure, then I will give you the details. The treasure is the first step in weakening the team. When you retrieve the treasure, bring it to me and I will show you the next step."

"You got it," he answered.

"You have five days to retrieve the treasure. I will meet you in the Temple of Life in South America in exactly five days. If you are late, it won't work. Get the treasure, and I'll get the four crystals." He got up and walked away. She smiled evilly.

In Washington, Calandra was dancing to a song on the radio in the office playroom. She was three years old. She was a good kid. We were worried about her, you know, with the attempted kidnapping. However, the criminals were caught and there hasn't been another attempt since. She didn't mind spending the entire day at the office while we worked on various projects. Then again there was an indoor and outdoor playground for her and she was supervised at all times.

I was busy working on some chemicals that were sent in by the Atlantis team. Heather was studying some weird dreams that she was having. She kept having dreams that didn't make sense to me but she believed there was a hidden message. They were basically the same dreams she had in paradise. She spent most of her time in the psych library but it didn't provide much help. She needed something to connect the dreams to the research. Chris was assigned by congress to create new time traveling laws. He was studying the various laws that already existed and working with other countries to make the best possible laws.

Steph was interested in studying the Atlantean language so she spent time researching in the language library. William was busy studying the history of various things because he couldn't come up with anything else. Krissy was working for a new food company, taste testing the food from various time periods.

I went into the playroom and picked Calandra up from dancing. "What are you dancing to," I asked her. She pointed to the radio. "Oh," I responded, "can you be good for a little while? I need to go check on mommy." She squirmed and tried to get down because she wanted to dance. I gave her a kiss on the forehead and put her down.

"She'll be fine," the one babysitter said. "Don't worry." I walked out of the room and down the hall.

"TJ," Johnson yelled, "the President wants you to report the findings of Atlantis in a paper to him."

"Ok," I answered. "When does he want it?"

"As soon as possible," he replied. I continued to walk down the hall. I bumped into a person I never saw before. He was tall with real dark hair. He had brown eyes. He was wearing jeans and a black leather jacket. His hair was gelled and shiny. He looked like he was a little older than us. He had an innocent face and smile.

"Oh," he said, "excuse me."

"Are you new," I asked. "I haven't seen you around before."

"Yeah," he responded, "I'm the new manager at the babysitting department. My name is David."

"Oh," I said, "I'm TJ, nice to meet you." We shook hands and then I continued on my way. Chris got off the elevator in front of me.

"I came up with a new law," he told me. "All machines have to have inspections to make sure their tracking devices work."

"Sounds good," I replied. "But I really have to check on Heather." I continued to walk down the hall.

"Also," he continued to follow me, "what if we make it mandatory for the person to register the time period they are going to with the government? And they have to tell us how long they are going for and the exact dates. They also have to give a reason."

"Great," I replied as I continued to walk toward the psych library. When I got to the main doors of the library I stopped. Chris stopped behind me. I turned around and looked at him. "Go down to your floor and do work," I told him. "I have plenty of stuff to do myself."

"Cool," he replied. He walked away. I opened the door and went in. The psych library was strange. It was a normal library but it had some weird equipment. I saw Heather sitting at a table reading books. I walked over and sat down.

"Did you find anything," I asked.

"Well," she responded, "you know how I had those dreams of a person stealing a treasure chest filled with gold and then I saw five great temples?"

"Yeah," I replied, "what do the books say?"

"They say that the treasure is something close to me. Something I interact with everyday. They say that the temples could be something that I am scared of. I realize that I am afraid of Poseidon's temple but that was one. What about the other four?"

"What did these temples look like?"

"They were all giant structures, very similar to castles, only they each had there own characteristic. The book also said that characteristics could be the personalities of the people around me. There are five teammates around me everyday. You, Krissy, Chris, Steph, and William. But why would I fear you and the team?"

"I don't know but maybe you will figure it out." I grabbed her hand and rubbed it. "What did the person that stole the treasure look like."

"He was ugly. Big built and dark, dark hair. His eyes were black and he was very mysterious. The book says it could be someone near me that I haven't met. So I'm guessing someone is going to try to steal my money. It is someone that I haven't met yet, but I will, and I will be friends with them."

"Well, I don't know what to tell you. Just keep your eyes and ears open. I have been having a weird feeling. That is never a good omen."

"Well you can't change your destiny." I kissed her and walked out of the library.

CHAPTER TWO

"Go in the temple and get me the crystal from the altar," the Psychic told some natives. She was in Egypt. Deep below the ground that she was standing on was the Temple of Earth. "You will be rewarded if you succeed." The two men entered the passageway that led to steps down into the temple. "Here's a map of the temple, you might find it useful." She threw the map to them and they walked down into the temple. It was dark and gloomy. They could hear water dripping. The steps seemed to go on forever. The men grabbed candles from the cave-like walls and continued down the steps.

When they got to the bottom of the steps they stopped. Through the candle light they could see they were in the main chamber. It was mostly all marble and gold. There were poles from the floor that went to the ceiling. On the wall in front of the men were signs with writing on them. One of the men walked over to the wall to read the writing. "You might want to look at this," he said. "That there woman is trying to cheat us. This says 'The Temple of Earth is guarded by the Terra Warriors. He who disturbs the crystal will be shaken from the face of the Earth."

"You don't really believe in that superstition," the other man said. "Do you?"

"I don't know what to think," the man replied, "but we are down in the Temple of Earth and until today I didn't even know it existed. So I don't know what to believe anymore. Maybe it is right, or maybe it is wrong. I don't know."

"Well, I think we should continue on our quest," the other man continued, "she said we will be rewarded."

"Yeah, but she didn't tell us what are reward is. It could be death."

"I don't think so. Stop being such a baby." They walked through the only door in the main room and that was to their right. This took them into a smaller room with a huge throne. Aside of the throne was a statue of the Earth Fairy. Around her were mountains and other 'earthly' features. To the left was another door. They walked through it and inside was a huge room. In the middle of the room there was an altar.

"That's it," one said, "that's the altar with the crystal." Just then they heard whispers all around them.

"I don't think we should be doing this."

"You are such a baby. There is nothing here. It's been dead for millions of years."

"What about the omen?"

"The only 'oh man' I know is the one we're going to be saying when we don't get the reward if we don't get her the crystal." He started to laugh.

"There is nothing funny about getting killed by ancient spirits." The other guy ignored him and started walking toward the altar. "Don't do it! You'll be sorry!" The whispers grew louder. They started to make sense.

"Free me from my grave," the whispers were getting louder, "open the chest and get the crystal. Wake me up and let me run. You will be rewarded."

"See," the man who was into it said, "we are going to be rewarded by the temple if we open the chest."

"Yeah, by death," the other replied. They walked over to the altar. The man who wasn't afraid opened the chest.

"AAAAHHHHH!" the whisper said in relief to be free. "Touch the crystal." The man reached in and grabbed the crystal from the chest. He picked it up and looked at it. It was green and had an Earth in the middle of it.

"This could be worth some money," he said. Suddenly the temple started to shake and the door they came in the room through, was blocked by a giant rock. There was another door on the other side of the room. The guys ran through the door to find themselves on a thin, narrow passage way made of rock that was over a giant gap.

"See," the other man said, "I told you. You shouldn't have touched the crystal." They started to walk slowly across the path. Then they heard some noises behind them. They looked back and saw some Terra Warriors. "Run!!!!!" They started to run quickly across the path. The Terra Warriors were green and had a mask on their face. When they got across the path the guys ran out the door. They were in the entrance room. They started up the steps to the surface. The cave was collapsing. They made it to the surface and they could hear the warriors behind them. The psychic was waiting for them.

"Give me the crystal," she said, "then I will help and reward you." The man handed her the crystal and she shot a wave of psychic energy at them and they fell back down the steps and the cave collapsed. The psychic held the crystal up and laughed evilly.

CHAPTER THREE

Heather met me in my office at about five o'clock. "Are you ready to leave?"

"Yeah, in a second," I replied. I grabbed my stuff and threw it in my bag and we walked out of my office. We walked to the playroom to get Calandra. Calandra was playing on the slide with one of the sitters. The sitters were all young girls. They were all probably our age or younger.

"Are you ready," Heather asked Calandra as she caught her coming down the slide. Calandra shook her head yes. She didn't talk much, she could, she just didn't like to. Heather picked her up and gave her a kiss. "You're getting too big," Heather told her. We walked to the door. "Say bye, we'll see you tomorrow." Calandra waved to the sitters.

"Goodnight," I said.

"Goodnight," they replied. We walked to the elevator and went in. I pushed the ground floor button. David was standing there.

"So you two are heading home for the night," he said.

"Yes," I replied.

"Hi, I'm Heather," she told him.

"I'm David," he replied, "the new babysitting department manager." She smiled at him.

"I hope to see you around sometime," she continued, "maybe we could talk." I looked at her trying to figure out what she was doing. When we got to the ground floor we got off. Johnson was in the lobby. We hurried past so he wouldn't see us but didn't succeed.

"Wait," Johnson yelled, "you didn't give me the paper for the President."

"I'll finish it tomorrow," I replied, "I'm going home. My job is done at five and it is five-fifteen. Good night." We walked out of the building. Chris, Krissy, William, and Steph worked till four. They start at eight and we start at nine so that Calandra can sleep in. Johnson and the other scientist work until seven and the guards have shifts throughout the night. Just because we get done at five doesn't mean we don't have to come back in the night. If it is needed we have to come back.

We got in the car and drove away. "Do you want to go out to dinner," I asked Heather. We hadn't been out to dinner in a while and there was a really good restaurant just down the road.

"Supper," Calandra said in baby talk, "out, McDonalds." Heather smiled and so did I.

"No," I said, "The restaurant that you like." She giggled with happiness.

"Yeah," Heather replied, "why not?"

"Call the others on your cell phone," I continued, "maybe they'll meet us." Heather pulled her cell phone from her purse and dialed. She informed the others to meet us there. They agreed. We pulled into the parking lot and parked. We got out and went into the restaurant.

"How many," the waitress asked.

"Six adults and a toddler," I answered.

"Right this way," she signaled for us to follow. We followed her to the table and sat down. The others joined us about five minutes later. We ordered our drinks and then our dinners.

"So," I said, "this would be a good time to discuss what we found on the research we have been doing."

"I'll start," Krissy responded, "I have been researching the food of various time periods. I must say that it is all very delicious. I have tried a lot of food. However, I like our food the best."

"You like anything," Chris replied.

"No one asked you," Krissy told Chris.

"Ok, your turn Chris," I said.

"I created a few new laws," Chris started, "they are as follows. First, all machines must have inspections to make sure they are working properly. Second, all machines that leave must register with us where they are going, what they are going for, and how long the trip is. Third, they are not allowed to leave with any weapons or equipment that might cause problems. Finally, if it is a group bigger than six, they must have a chaperone from the government with them."

"Sounds great," I responded, "but where do we get the chaperones?"

"We train people to be chaperones," he answered.

"Doesn't that cost too much money," Heather asked.

"Well we do have money in our account," he continued. "Why can't we use that?"

"And what if we have another mission that requires new technology," I questioned him.

"We won't have another mission anytime soon," he responded. "And if we do, we won't need new technology."

"You can look into it," I told him, "but I'm not guaranteeing anything. It might cost too much money, the kind that we don't have. It will also mean more work for us. I don't think I like it."

"Well isn't it up to Johnson and the rest of the team," he said.

"Look," I responded angrily, "I am not saying no. I just said I won't make any promises."

"So William," Heather cut in, "did you find anything interesting?" She knew she had to stop us from arguing.

"No, not really," he responded.

"I found a lot of weird stuff on my dreams," Heather told us, "and it's starting to make sense."

"What exactly was your dream," Krissy asked.

"My dreams," Heather replied, "have been really strange. They start with five temples and the elements; Earth, Fire, Wind, Water, and Life. Then they show a mysterious woman and a real ugly man. I always hear Calandra crying in the background. And in some of the dreams, I see the four of you, all except TJ, die in weird ways."

"What do the books say," Chris asked.

"They just give me pieces," she responded, "I have to piece it together." When we finished eating I paid and then we left.

"From now on," I told Heather, "when you wake up from a dream you should write down exactly what happened."

"I have been doing that," she said. Calandra was sleeping in the back. Heather was singing along with a song on the radio. Just then a car pulled out behind me from a dark ally. It turned its lights on. I kept an eye on the car as it continued to catch up to us. It kept coming closer.

"What the hell," I said.

"Hey," Heather corrected me, "not in front of Calandra."

"This car is getting awfully close…," I started. Before I could finish the car had bumped into the back of us.

"What's going on," Heather said in fear as she looked back.

Calandra woke up crying. Then it ran into us again.

"What do they want," I asked.

"Hurry," Heather screamed.

"I'm going to pull over and see what there problem is," I told her.

"No," she said, "just get us home." Then the car came up alongside us and ran into the side of our car. It knocked me off the road but I swerved back up onto the road. "Who would be following us," Heather continued. "Knock it off, there's a baby in here."

"They can't hear you," I told her. The car ran into the side of us again. This time I was able to keep us on the road. Calandra was crying in the backseat.

"I have to go back with her," Heather told me.

"Just be careful," I replied. She unbuckled and started to climb into the back seat. The car ran into us again and Heather hit her head against the window.

"Mommy," Calandra cried.

"Are you ok," I asked Heather.

"Yeah," she answered, "just pay attention to the road." It was really dark and starting to rain. I stepped on the gas to try to get passed this car. The car got behind me and sped up also. They ran into the back of us again. Then I saw one of the guys in the car climb out onto its roof.

"Oh my God," I screamed, "he's getting out of the car and he has a gun." He fired the gun at our tire. He missed.

"Hurry," Heather screamed.

"I'm trying." We were heading down the road to our house. I made a right turn.

"Where are you going," Heather asked. "Take us home."

"Do you want them to follow us home," I questioned already knowing the answer. I opened the glove compartment on the passenger side of the car. I pulled out the laser that was in there. I handed it to Heather.

"What's this for," she asked.

"Shine it in the driver's eyes," I responded, "when they get closer." The car came close and she shined it in the drivers eyes. The car swerved and went off the road and flipped over. I sped up before they could get out of the car. Then I continued on home.

CHAPTER FOUR

When we got home Heather got Calandra out of the car. I opened the door to the house and turned the lights on. Heather took Calandra right up to her room because she was sleeping again. Then she came back down and sat next to me on the couch. "Who would try to kill us," she asked. "And how did they know it was us?"

"I don't know," I replied, "maybe we were just in the wrong place at the wrong time." She laid her head on my shoulder. I ran my fingers through her hair. She looked up at me and I kissed her.

The next morning, when I woke up, we were still both on the couch. We never made it up to bed the night before; we fell asleep right there on the couch. Heather felt me move and she woke up. We got up and took our showers and got Calandra ready. Then we headed to work. When we got there we took Calandra to the babysitting department. The sitters were all waiting for her and they smiled when we walked in. Calandra was excited to play this morning so Heather put her down and she ran right for the slide.

"Good morning," the one sitter said. Her name was Stacy and she had blonde hair with brown eyes.

"Good morning," Heather and I replied.

"Where's David," Heather asked. "Isn't he supposed to start today?"

"Yes," she answered, "but he called off sick."

"What's the matter," I asked.

"He was in a car accident last night," Stacy continued.

"Oh," Heather responded, "that's terrible."

"He should be in tomorrow," Stacy continued. Now I had a real weird feeling in my gut. We walked out of the room and down the hall toward our offices.

"That is really weird," I said, "he had a car accident."

"So," Heather replied, "they happen."

"You don't think it was him," I asked.

"No," she answered, "there are many car accidents every night in this city."

"True," I continued, "but it seems too weird."

"Just relax," she told me. She gave me a kiss. "I have to go continue my research."

"Alright. I'll be in the Library of Science or with one of the other team members." She went into the library. I on the other hand, took the elevator down to the second floor to talk to Chris and Steph. They were sitting in their snack room when I went in.

"Hey," Chris said. "What's up?"

"I need to talk," I told him. "You know after dinner last night?"

"Yeah," he replied, "what about it?"

"On our way home we almost got run off the road by a mysterious car. Heather shined a laser in the driver's eyes and the car flipped over in a ditch."

"Who was it," Steph asked.

"I don't know," I answered, "but the weirdest part is that David, the new babysitting department manager, was in an accident last night."

"Why is that weird," Chris asked. "There are accidents all over this city with the way these people drive."

"I don't know," I told him, "it just seems to fit together so easily."

"I don't know what to tell you," Steph continued. "I don't know what it is." I got up and walked to the elevator.

Meanwhile, deep inside a Hawaiian volcano, the psychic had a few natives down in the fire temple trying to retrieve the crystal. The natives walked into the main chamber and saw the chest. They walked up to the chest and looked at it. "Open the chest," a voice came through the room. One of the natives did exactly as he was told. He opened the chest. "Touch the crystal," the voice continued. The native picked the crystal out of the chest. "AAAAAHHHHH," the voice cried in relief. The natives smiled and were happy that they were going to be getting rewarded. The temple started to shake.

"Hurry," the one native told the others. They started running through the temple. When they got to the entrance the psychic was waiting for them.

"Give me the crystal," she told them. The native threw her the crystal and she caught it. She started laughing and then shot lava at the natives and they fell backwards into the volcano.

CHAPTER FIVE

Later that afternoon, I was sitting in my office playing solitaire on my computer. There was a knock at my door and I looked. It was Stacy from the babysitting department. "What's up," I asked her.

"David just called me," she replied, "he's my boyfriend. Anyway, he wants to know if you and Heather would like to go out to dinner tomorrow night. You can bring Calandra if you want."

"I'll have to ask Heather," I told her. "We'll let you know later today, when we pick Calandra up."

"Ok," she responded as she walked away. I knew this was getting a little too weird. Why would David be trying to make friends with us and was it just a coincidence that he was in a car accident last night? I didn't think so, but Heather did. She is the one with the dream, she would know.

Meanwhile, Heather was working on figuring her dreams out in the Library of Psychology. Steph went in and sat down at the table with her. "So," Steph said, "I heard you were attacked last night."

"Yeah," Heather replied, "it was scary. Calandra was in the backseat."

"Well, I'm just glad everyone is ok."

"Me too."

"You don't look good," Steph told Heather. "Are you feeling ok?"

"I just don't feel right," Heather answered, "I don't know if I'm tired or what."

"Too much stress," Steph responded. "And getting attacked last night didn't help. Or maybe it is more."

"No, I think I'm just tired," Heather continued.

"Chris and I are going to grab some lunch," Steph told Heather. "What do you want?"

"Just get me a salad," Heather replied, "with fat-free ranch dressing."

"Alright," Steph said, "I need to ask TJ." She walked up to my office and knocked on my door.

"Come in," I said. She opened the door and peered in.

"Chris and I are going for lunch," she told me. "What can I get you?"

"I'll have a hoagie," I responded, "with some chips and a soda." I gave her money for Heather and I. "And get Calandra a chicken finger platter with French fries," I told her as she walked away. She gave me a thumbs up. Heather came in.

"I'm going to get Calandra ready for lunch," she told me. "Then after lunch I'm going home. I don't feel good." I got up and walked over to her. She put her arms around me. "I'm worried about Calandra." I went to kiss her but Krissy and William knocked on the door.

"Cut the mushy stuff," Krissy said, "it's gross."

"What do you want," I asked.

"To let you know to get the lunch room ready," Krissy answered.

"Why can't you," I continued.

"Because we don't feel like it," she snapped. They walked away.

"You get Calandra," I told Heather. "I'll get the lunch room ready." She walked to the babysitting department and I took the elevator down to the ground floor. I got plates out and stuff. Heather came in with Calandra.

"Daddy," Calandra yelled as Heather put her down. Calandra ran over to me and I picked her up and hugged her. Heather got the booster seat from the counter and put it on one of the chairs. Then I put Calandra in the chair.

"Are you hungry," Heather asked Calandra. She shook her head yes.

"I ordered you chicken fingers," I told her. She smiled. Heather sat down next to her. Chris and Steph came in with the food and Krissy and William followed. Not far behind came Johnson. Johnson tapped Calandra on the head when he came in. Krissy grabbed her chicken sandwich and started eating. William started eating his steak sandwich. I gave Heather her salad. Chris handed Calandra her chicken fingers.

"No," Heather yelled, "you have to cut them up and let them cool. They are too hot."

"Alright," Chris responded, "I didn't know." I took the chicken fingers and started cutting them up for Calandra. Chris and Steph sat down and started eating. Johnson grabbed a piece of pizza and took it from the room. I put Calandra's meal in front of her and she started eating. I started to unwrap my hoagie.

"TJ," Johnson said from the doorway, "you might want to have a look at this." I wrapped my hoagie and put it in the refrigerator. Then I walked out to the main lobby.

"I wish he would just eat," Heather said. "People can never leave him alone for more than two seconds."

"She's grouchy," Chris whispered to Steph.

"She doesn't feel good," Steph whispered back. Johnson showed me the paper.

TEMPLES BEING ATTACKED

As of late two temples were attacked. One in Africa and one in Hawaii. In both, the crystals they held were stolen. The temples are part of the set of temples that are called the Temples of the Elements. The one in Africa was the Temple of Earth and the one in Hawaii was the Temple of Fire. The crystals of each element are believed to possess some kind of magical powers that were used to create the world. Police and government officials are trying to figure out who stole the crystals and why.

I handed him the paper and shrugged my shoulder. "I'll look it up," I told him, "but I can't promise anything." He shook his head yes. I took the elevator up to the third floor. Then I headed right for the Library of Science. I started searching.

Meanwhile, high on top of a mountain in Germany, some natives were running from the Aer Warriors. They stole the crystal and were now running for the entrance. When they got to the entrance they gave the psychic the crystal and she shot a gust of wind at them. They flew backwards into the temple and she shot a blast that closed the entrance to the temple.

CHAPTER SIX

Heather came into the library where I was sitting. "Why didn't you eat," she asked. "What could possibly be more important than your health?"

"Johnson showed me some breaking news," I replied, "I needed to get cracking on it."

"What's going to crack is your head when you pass out from not eating and hit your head."

"I'm fine, I can take care of myself." I smiled at her.

"I guess this means you won't take me home, right?"

"I want to stay and get this done."

"Did you forget that I told you I didn't feel good?"

"Oh, yeah, I did forget."

"AAAHHHH!" She got really upset. "Why does work have to be so important to you? Do you care that I am so sick that I was in the bathroom for ten minutes after I got done eating? No you don't because you were here, working. Steph and Chris took Calandra back to the babysitters because I was so sick." She stormed out of the library.

"Heather, wait, I'll take you home." I slammed my head on the table. "Why are you so sick," I yelled after her. She came storming back.

"Do you remember the night on the couch a few weeks ago," she asked, "when we didn't go up to bed?"

"Yeah," I responded, "why?"

"Because of that night, I am sick," she continued.

"How," I asked.

"I'm pregnant again," she answered.

"Oh my God," I gasped, "I can't believe it. I'm so happy."

"Are you," she asked. "Why, so you can push this to the side too, for work?"

"Hold on," I told her, "let me pack up. We're going home." She agreed and walked away. I closed the books I was working with and ran to my office. I grabbed the papers off my desk and threw them in my bag. I grabbed my keys from my desk drawer and locked up my office. I ran to the sitters and grabbed Calandra and then met Heather in the hall by her office. We took the elevator down to the ground floor.

"Where are you going," Johnson asked. "Did you get me my information?"

"Not yet," I told him, "we're going home. Heather doesn't feel good."

"Don't push it," Johnson said. "You two take advantage of your job way too much." Heather looked at me.

"What are you going to do," Heather asked, "fire us?"

"Maybe," Johnson replied, "you won't leave us any other choice."

"I'll come back as soon as I take her home," I told him.

"What," Heather asked in shock. I pulled her arm and led her out of the building and to the car. I drove away. "What do you mean you'll go back," Heather wanted to know.

"I have to," I replied, "he's threatening us with our jobs."

"So what," she said.

"So we need the money," I told her. Just then I saw something in the middle of the road in front of us. There was a car pulled over to the side. I slowed to a stop and got out of the car. I looked around to see what was going on. Somebody was laying in the middle of the road. The person that was laying there sat up and started firing a gun at me. Heather screamed.

"Get back in the car," she yelled. I ran back into the car and drove off. The car that was pulled over on the side pulled out behind me. "HURRY!" I took a side street and turned to head back to the office.

"We're going back to the office," I told Heather.

"What," she cried out. "Why?"

"We have reinforcements there," I continued. The car followed us. When we got to the office I drove the car down into the underground parking lot. I closed the garage door before the car could follow us in. I hurried to get Calandra out of the car and we ran into the building.

"Are we safe," Heather asked.

"I don't know," I told her. "I don't know if they will follow us in." We were in the basement. "Alright," I said, "keep Calandra here." I showed her to hide in the equipment room. I grabbed a gun from the shelf and ran out of the room. I took the steps to the ground floor. When I got there I pointed my gun around and the tourists that were there screamed. Johnson looked at me.

"What are you doing," he asked.

"We were followed here," I told him, "they tried to kill us again." The one guard came over and grabbed the gun from my hand.

"You won't be needing that," he told me, "we are here." They searched the building to make sure that there was no one in it that would threaten us. There wasn't anyone suspicious even near the building.

CHAPTER SEVEN

"I'm telling you," I told the guards, "someone followed us. Are you sure they didn't come in after us?"

"The only person that came in here in the last fifteen minutes was David from the babysitting department and he is authorized to be here." I walked away, still not comfortable with the occurring situation, but what was I going to do. I had no proof of who it was. I took the elevator back down to the basement and walked into the equipment room.

"Was there anyone there," Heather asked.

"No," I replied, "not according to the guards. Not that that means anything."

"Did anyone come into the building," Heather continued to ponder.

"Yeah," I answered, "just David."

"But that is not suspicious," she said.

"Or is it," I asked her. "Maybe he is after Calandra. If you had a dream about someone we got to know stealing our treasure, then maybe it is David trying to kidnap Calandra. It works."

"Maybe he just happens to be at the wrong place at the wrong time. What proof do we have that it is him," Heather continued.

"What proof do we have that it's not," I asked. She shrugged her shoulder and then we left for home.

Meanwhile Stacy and David were sitting in the babysitting department talking. "Do you think they caught on yet," Stacy asked David.

"I don't know but they have to be suspicious," he replied. "And I only have two more days to get the kid and get to South America."

"Why don't you just take her when they drop her off here," Stacy demanded to know, "it would be a lot easier."

"Yes it would," David replied, "but I thought I could eliminate the leaders while I was at it."

"Well you can't," Stacy told him, "so just get the kid and run. Then you will be able to beat the team when you have the power of the elements behind you."

"I'll get her tomorrow," David responded, "as soon as they drop her off. Then I'll fly to South America. They'll never know and they'll have to embark on a study before they can chase me. By that time, I'll have the elements backing me."

"Then be here on time," she told him, "and don't try anything tonight. They aren't going to dinner with us."

"Tomorrow it is," David concluded.

"I'll call Karma," Stacy said, "she'll be prepared." They smiled evilly at each other.

The next morning came quickly. "Did you sleep ok," I asked Heather as I poured each of us a cup of coffee and sat down at our kitchen table. She sat down across for me.

"Yeah," she replied, "except that I had a dream that when we went to pick Calandra up one day at the baby-sitting department, she wasn't there."

"What do you mean she wasn't there," I asked.

"She was gone and the babysitters had no idea of where she was," Heather continued. "But it didn't seem to be connected to the other dreams." We sat there silently trying to piece all of the dreams together. Heather went to get Calandra up and I took my shower. After we were all ready, we headed to work and dropped Calandra off. David and Stacy were the only ones there. Then, Heather and I both headed to the Library of Psychology to work on the dreams together.

Meanwhile, up in the babysitting department, Stacy looked at David. "Now, she told him, "before the other employees get here. The rest of the team is coming in late today. This is your best opportunity."

"Alright," he said, "you distract them and I'll sneak her out of here."

"Good," Stacy said, "you have a plan. But don't forget the

239

equipment."

"Right," David responded as he picked Calandra up. Stacy ran down to the psych library and came in to talk to us.

"I am quitting," she told us, "I turned in my papers." I looked at Heather.

David made his way to the basement to get some of our equipment. He walked into the equipment room to find Johnson standing there.

"What are you doing down here," Johnson asked, "you are not authorized to be…" Before he could finish, David hit him across the back of the head with a metal pipe that was laying on one of the shelves. Calandra started crying.

"Shut up," David told her as he put her down. He started collecting some equipment. Calandra walked over to Johnson.

"Push the alarm," Johnson told Calandra as he pointed to the wall where the alarm was, "mommy and daddy will come." Calandra ran over to the alarm and pushed it. David turned around quickly knowing he was in trouble.

Upstairs in the psych library the alarm flashed for an unauthorized person in the equipment room. I looked at Heather and ran out the door. Heather followed. We took off down the steps toward the basement.

David grabbed the time belts and Calandra and ran out of the door and down the hall. He ran out into the underground parking garage.

Heather and I ran into the equipment room and Johnson was just getting up. "David has kidnapped Calandra," Johnson yelled, "hurry!" But before he could finish Heather and I were down the hall. David got into our car with the copy of the keys he made. He started it up. We ran toward the car. He started to drive away so I jumped onto the car and climbed to the roof but the wind blew me off. David stepped on the gas and sped out of the garage and out of sight. Heather ran over to me and held onto me.

"That was my dream," she said, "the chain of events are starting to come true." We walked back into the equipment room and met Dr. Johnson. Heather and I got into our warrior outfits. I grabbed the usual equipment from the shelves.

"Where are the time belts," Heather asked.

"David stole them," Johnson answered.

"What does he want with Calandra and the time belts," Heather cried as she dropped to her knees crying.

"The secret," I told her, "lies in you, in your dreams." She looked at me knowing that I was ready for a battle. She had a look of concern on her face but she knew we had no other choice, our little girl was in the hands of evil people. "Let's go," I told her, "no time to lose." She stood up.

"Don't you want to call the others," Johnson asked.

"No," I answered, "we don't need them."

"All we need," Heather said, "is our parental instinct."

"Wait," I continued, "Stacy must have been a part of this." I ran up the steps to the third floor and caught Stacy trying to leave the building. I grabbed a hold of her and pushed her against the wall. "Where is he," I asked her.

"Who," she responded.

"You know who," I told her, "don't play games. You can't protect him." I took her down the hall and into my office where Heather met us.

CHAPTER EIGHT

"I don't know what you are talking about," Stacy pleaded.

"Don't even try that," I told her. "You know what he wants with Calandra."

"I can't tell you," she said, "I promised him." Johnson and a few guards walked in.

"Take her to our holding place for criminals," I told the guards, "until she decides to talk." They carried her down to the basement where we had a jail cell to hold criminals.

"Can I help you in anyway," Johnson asked.

"Yeah," I responded, "how did he get a job here?"

"We cleared his background," Johnson replied.

"What is his full name," I asked.

"David Koorb," Johnson answered. I ran over to my computer and typed in David Koorb. The computer didn't have any files on him.

"There are no files on him," I told Johnson. "How did you clear his background?"

"One of my secretaries told me he was clear," he replied.

"Which secretary was it," Heather asked.

"Mary," Johnson answered her.

"She is new," Heather told him, "she probably thought that if there were no files he was clear." I slammed my hand down on my desk.

"You let a criminal in to our building and didn't even know it," I yelled. "Since when do we let a god damn new secretary check a background on someone watching our daughter? What the hell were you thinking? What kind of agency is this turning into?"

"A very unprepared one," Heather answered. Johnson looked at her in sadness. I clicked the button that searched for similar names. Three hundred and forty-eight thousand came back.

"How am I supposed to choose a name from 348,000," I asked.

"Koorb," Heather replied, "that sounds familiar. Why?"

"Maybe from the dream," I told her. She closed her eyes and images flashed before her. She saw a paper sitting on a desk by a mirror. She looked into the mirror and saw David with the paper saying skoorB. Then she looked down at the desk and saw the paper. It read 'David Brooks.'

"That's it," she said, "it's Tyler and Kelly's brother. His name is David Brooks, I saw it in a dream memory just now."

"Good job," I told her, "keep thinking about the dreams, maybe it will lead us to something." I typed in David Brooks and a file came up. But the file said he didn't have any siblings. "It says he doesn't have any siblings." Heather closed her eyes again.

"He's the oldest," she told me, "and he wants to continue the family business of trying to control time."

"Keep looking," I told her, "you're really onto something." Chris and the others walked into my office.

"What's going on," Chris asked. I explained what happened.

"Stay here," I told him, "help Johnson. This is for Heather and I only."

"Right," he responded.

"I'll start making new time belts," Johnson told us, "just in case."

"I know where he is going," Heather told me, "to the airport."

"Let's go," I told her. We ran down to the basement and got the team's motorcycles. We drove to the airport. We ran into the building and to the first desk that we saw.

"David Brooks," Heather told the lady at the desk, "where is he going?"

"I am not allowed to give information out like that," she responded.

"We are the Time Warriors," I said as we showed her our badges, "he is a criminal." She typed his name in.

"Argentina," she told us, "U.S. Air flight 208." We ran down the terminals to find the right one.

"U.S. Air flight 208 is now taking off," the intercom said. I ran to the nearest desk and flashed my badge.

"Get them to hold all planes from taking off," I told her. Then we took off toward the U.S. Air terminals.

"All planes are being asked to delay take off due to a governmental request," the lady announced over the intercom, "please remain in place." David stood up from his seat on the plane when her heard the announcement. The plane was already going down the runway.

"You have clearance to take off," the controllers told the pilot, "ignore the announcement." The plane took off. Heather and I made it to the terminal in time to see the plane lift into the air. Heather watched in horror as the plane disappeared into the clouds. Tears started to stream down her face. I, on the other hand, was ready for a fight. I took off running back to the first desk I went to.

"Where in South America are they going," I asked the lady. The lady ignored me and walked away.

"Let's go," Heather told me, "we can track them from headquarters."

"Right," I responded.

CHAPTER NINE

Back at headquarters, Heather and I were sitting in my office. I started paging through some of the psych books that we borrowed from the library. "There has to be a clue in your dreams that will tell us the next step," I told Heather.

"If I didn't dream it already, I probably will," she said.

"But I still can't figure out how our three year old daughter can help them," I continued. "It just doesn't make sense."

"Well there is certainly a reason why they needed her," Heather told me. "We just have to figure out what they are going to use her for."

"Then maybe we should head to South America," I continued, "to find them and get her back."

"It won't be that easy," Heather responded, "they plan that we will go after them. That's what they want. It's like a distraction from something. They captured her to distract us from their real plan."

"I don't think they captured our daughter to distract us," I said.

"Maybe," Heather replied, "maybe not, we don't know what they are doing." Chris walked into my office.

"Did you figure anything out," he asked.

"No," I told him, "we're still working on it."

"Why don't you let us help," he asked Heather and I. "Maybe if all six of us worked on it, we would be able to figure it out."

"We don't need you four," I told him, "Johnson does. He needs you to be prepared for the next mission." Chris looked at Heather. Heather nodded in agreement with me.

"Alright," Chris continued, "if you want it that way. But don't say we didn't offer." He walked out in disgust.

"Let's book a flight to South America," I told Heather, "for as soon as possible."

"Alright," she responded, "if you really think we should be running out after them."

"I do," I told her, "I think it is our only option. Our daughter is out there with those criminals and we need to get her back."

"And you are sure this is the best way," she asked.

"Yes," I told her, "I am positive." I picked up the phone and called the airport. As I was dialing, Johnson walked in and handed Heather two time belts.

"That was fast," Heather said.

"I have a group to help me now," Johnson responded, "and they are experienced at making them so it goes fast." Johnson nodded at me and walked out. Heather fixed her pants and shirt and then clipped the belt around her waist. Then she came over behind me and clipped the belt around my waist. She smiled at me and kept her hands on my belt. After I was done booking the flight I put the phone down and sat down on my desk.

"I hope Calandra is ok," Heather told me.

"She'll be fine," I comforted her, "she has our genes for intelligence and endurance."

"That's true," Heather agreed.

"But we still have to battle," I told her.

CHAPTER TEN

Heather and I walked into the airport and looked around. Our plane was scheduled to leave in about two hours but we needed to make it through the checkpoints. We put our bags down and walked over to the desk. Heather followed me over. Our bags had all of the equipment that we needed that couldn't be carried on our belts, plus some clothes. I had a computer and tracking device in my bag. Heather stood next to me as the lady prepared to check us in. "I have a bad feeling about this," Heather told me, "I think we are walking into a trap."

"We're fine," I replied, "we'll be prepared. Where are the bags?"

"Over there," she answered as she pointed to them. I looked and they were fine. The lady was taking her time with something on the computer. I was hoping she would speed it up.

"Have a seat," she told me, "it will be about an hour and a half before we get to your plane."

"But we only have two hours," I told her.

"I know," she responded, "but there are other planes not checked in and they leave sooner."

"Alright," I said as I walked away and Heather followed. Heather sat down and I grabbed the bags and then joined her. I kept looking around for something suspicious but the airport was so crowded that nothing stood out. Heather still insisted that she had a bad feeling about this. I leaned back and closed my eyes.

An hour and a half later, Heather was washing her hands in the bathroom when she suddenly flashed into a vision. She saw me sitting by myself in a crowded area, with bags under my seat. I was sleeping and someone snuck up and stole the bags. She snapped out of the vision and started to think what that meant. Then an older lady started washing her hands. "The equipment," Heather screamed. The older lady just looked at her, confused. Heather grabbed paper towels and ran out of the bathroom. She dried her hands quickly as she was running down the terminals back to where I was sitting. She threw the paper towels in a garbage can as she passed one. People were looking at her. Then someone hit her from behind. She turned around to find a woman with black hair standing there. She was dressed in all black. The woman slapped Heather in the face.

"Don't mess with time," the woman told Heather, "you are going to get hurt."

"Who are you," Heather asked.

"I am part of a group that is your worst nightmare," the woman answered, "you're about to learn that time is against you." Heather slapped her in the face and then kicked her in the stomach.

Meanwhile where I was sitting, five guys jumped through the glass in the roof and landed around me. People started screaming. I woke up to find them standing around me. One of them sprayed me with something and everything went black. Heather ran away from the girl she was fighting, and made her way back to me. By the time she got back to me, the guys left with the bags. She shook me and I woke up.

"The bags are gone," she told me, "and I was attacked by some weird woman that said she is from a group that is our worst nightmare. She also told me that we are going to learn that time is against us." I stood up and started looking around. They were no where in sight.

"Why would they want the equipment," I asked myself.

"They want to prevent us from tracking them," Heather answered. "I told you they are trying to distract us from something else. If we find them, we won't be distracted."

"Son of a bitch," I yelled.

"What," Heather asked.

"They have the tickets for the flight," I told her, "they were in my bag. Let's go." I took off running toward the terminal that our flight was leaving. Heather followed me pushing our way through the crowd. We got to a metal detector and ran through it and the guards were yelling to us.

We kept running, some of the guards chased after us.

"They have to be around here," Heather told me, "they didn't board yet."

"Yes they did," I told her, "they are about to take off."

"What do we do," she asked.

"Get your badge ready," I responded, "we're going to run onto the plane." We pulled our badges out. "Now," I yelled. We ran past the attendant at the boarding door and flashed our badges. We ran down the boarding tunnel toward the plane. They closed the door of the plane. It started to take off so I pulled my long shot out and grabbed a hold of Heather. I shot my long shot at the plane's tire and it hooked around the metal bar connected to the tire. Then we swung from the boarding tunnel to the tire and grabbed on. "Climb up," I told her, "quickly, before the landing gear goes in." We climbed up and into the storage area.

"Now what," she asked.

"We sit and wait until we arrive in South America," I replied. We sat down on some boxes that were nearby.

Meanwhile, deep in the Atlantic ocean, the psychic was in the process of stealing the crystal form the Temple of Water. The natives swam out of the temple and handed her the crystal. She shot a wave of water at them and they were pushed back into the temple. Then she blocked the door with boulders that were nearby. She surfaced and climbed onto her boat. "At last," she said, "I have the power of the four elements, combined with my psychic abilities. Now we will have no problem beating the warriors." She was now on her way to South America.

Back in Washington, Chris, Steph, William, Krissy, and Johnson were watching the news. "Today the last of the four temples, the Temple of Water, had its crystal stolen. We don't know where the temples are located but we know that the crystals were stolen because people around the world are getting visions of the robberies. All visions are connected with the mass destruction of the world. The next target may be the Temple of Life, but that is known to be only a myth."

"Heather's dreams involved the temples," Steph said.

"Yeah, and us," Chris replied.

"She must be getting the visions too," William added. "But what is it connected to?"

"I asked TJ to investigate but he got tied up in other priorities," Johnson told them, "maybe you four can look into it."

"Right," Chris said, "we're on it." The four of them went and got there warrior outfits on and grabbed equipment, then they headed to the Library of Science.

CHAPTER ELEVEN

"Look up anything that has to do with the four elements and creation of the Earth," Chris told Steph. "Look up the four elements and their temples," he told Krissy and William. "I'll look up the four elements and the destruction of the world." They broke up and started on their investigation into the elements. Johnson walked in and went over to Chris.

"I'll check around to see if I can find someone that has information on the elements," Johnson told Chris, "like an expert or something."

"Right," Chris responded, "good idea." Johnson walked out of the library. "Let's crack this case," Chris yelled to the others, "and help our leaders for once instead of them helping us." They spent hour upon hour trying to figure out what the elements had to do with anything. They made copies of or wrote down anything that seemed to be really important.

Johnson walked into his lab and sat down at his computer. He typed in 'experts' and then 'the four elements'. Hundreds of entries appeared from all around the world. "Jackpot," he yelled. He started going through the list.

Meanwhile, in the library, Steph found information on how the elements helped to create the Earth in some myths. Krissy and William started mapping the temples out room by room. Chris was looking into mythology of how the elements would cause the end of the world and why someone would want their power. Johnson walked into the library.

"Here is the name, address, and phone number of the lady that seems to be the biggest expert," Johnson told Chris. Chris looked at the paper and then at the group.

"It's time to pay Estelle Thompson a visit," Chris said, "she lives a few blocks from here." They walked out of the library and took the elevator to the ground floor. Then they walked down the street toward this lady's house. People on the street recognized that they were the warriors in their outfits and that meant trouble was brewing for the world again.

Chris knocked on Estelle's door. She opened the door. "How can I help you?"

"We are the Time Warriors," Chris told her, "we need you to tell us everything you know about the elements."

"Come in," she responded, "sit down and I will create an image for you." They all sat down and prepared to be enlightened. "There is darkness. A deep, cold, consistent darkness. Then out of the eternal darkness comes five small lights. One purple, one blue, one green, one red, and one gray. They meet and a ball of energy is formed. The ball of energy spins rapidly in the darkness shooting off light. When the ball of energy becomes a solid light the five lights reveal themselves as five creatures, almost fairy like, only much bigger than fairies. They are the five colors. They look down on their masterpiece. "Let's have a contest," the purple fairy said to the others. "Which ever one of us can create the most useful and successful adaptation to this ball will win."

"Ok," the other four agreed. The green fairy stepped forward. She threw her arms into the darkness and created a ball of green energy and light.

"With the power of Terra," she said, "I give the ball dirt." She shot the ball of energy at the object and it turned into a solid ball of dirt.

"Terra," the red one said, "I can give it a better contraption." He swung his arms into the air and created a red ball. He threw it at the ball of dirt and there was lava. Then he created another red ball and threw it into space. "Let there be light." The sun was created. The blue fairy stepped up. She threw a blue ball at the globe.

"Let there be water," she said, "with the power of Aqua."

"Then the water has to be recycled," the gray fairy said, "with the power of Aer I create oxygen and the atmosphere. I also give it weather." They all stepped back and looked as their new portrait took form. The green and brown land was split by water. There were white clouds in the picture. The sun shone down on the new masterpiece and heated it up.

"Then," the purple fairy said, "I give our new creation what it needs. Something to use everything you created. It is called 'life'." She shot a purple ball of energy at the spinning globe. "Now we call it EARTH, which means 'life'"

And for millions and millions of years the five elements lived on Earth in their temples. High in the mountains of Germany is the Temple of Air. In the west, somewhere in Hawaii, in a volcano is the Temple of Fire. In the middle of the Atlantic Ocean is the Temple of Water. Deep under the ground in Egypt is the Temple of Earth. And finally, deep in the jungles of South America is the Temple of Life. The element of life won the contest. She created this word 'KARMA' or destiny. She told the other elements that she had control over what happened on Earth. They believed her. However, she became greedy. She wanted control over the entire Earth and to get rid of the other elements. She created humans without the other elements knowing it. She led us on a quest to conquer the lands and temples of the four other elements. She trapped the four elements in four crystals and put them in an altar in her temple in South America. As long as she held those four elements, life would remain her play toy. However, humans decided that they didn't like her ruling them and so they destroyed her temple. She fled into hiding and was never seen again. The humans then controlled the Earth and life itself. They returned the four crystals to their rightful temples where they would be safe for all time."

"That is until now," Chris told her.

"What do you mean by that," she asked.

"The four crystals were stolen from the temples as of late," Steph replied, "that's why we are here."

"Why would someone want the crystals," William asked.

"My dear boy," Estelle said, "those crystals contain the elements themselves. Whomever holds the crystals has the power of the elements and can use it for whatever he or she wants."

"So you told us the creation of the Earth from the elements," Chris said, "why someone would want the crystals, and about where the temples are located. But what kind of damage could this power do if it got into the wrong hands?"

"The five elements used their powers in a good way to create the Earth and life," Estelle responded, "but if someone with a dark and evil heart was to hold the crystals, they could use the power for ultimate destruction of the world. If one was to combine the four powers in a dark and evil way, the result would be the effect of millions of nuclear bombs going of in one set place, yet it would cover the entire world."

"So," Chris recapped, "if someone was to use this for evil, it would be like setting off millions of nuclear bombs in one spot, but it would happen all around the world."

"Right," Estelle replied.

"So it would be like millions of nuclear bombs hitting every city in the world," Steph added.

"Yes," Estelle said, "but every city, town, village, and unpopulated area in the world."

"How could we beat the person that controlled these powers," Chris asked, "because that is our goal?"

"It would be impossible," Estelle answered.

"We don't give into impossible," Krissy told her.

"Then you would have to enter all four of the temples and beat the warriors that live there. They contain a necklace that has the same power and if you were to beat the warrior, the necklace would belong to you and you could master its power. But that would be a task in itself."

"Then," Chris told the others, "I don't know about you, but it looks like I'm going to have to kick some major elemental ass."

CHAPTER TWELVE

"What do you mean you don't know where the man went," I asked, "it's not that hard." I was really angry with the flight attendants for not knowing where David went even though I described him to her four times.

"Sir," she replied, "I told you, hundreds of people walked off the planed. I really don't know who you are talking about." Heather signaled me to give up.

"Fine," I said in disgust, "thank you." I walked away. "How can they not know where David went?"

"Lots of people walked off the plane," Heather explained, "they can't keep track of them."

"How do we find our daughter when we don't know where they went and even worse, we don't have our equipment."

"We'll have to follow my dreams," Heather replied.

"But do your dreams tell you where they are headed," I asked.

"Yeah," she replied, "to the Temple of Life."

"How do we get there?"

"I don't know. My dreams didn't explain that yet." We started to walk out of the airport. When we got outside our rental car was waiting for us. We had no idea where we were going so we just drove.

"I wish we had some kind of clue," I told Heather.

"Make a right at this light," she told me.

"What," I responded, "why?"

"Just do it," she told me, "I'm having a day dream and it is explaining the way to me." I made the right. "Follow this road to the end." I did as she told me. We came to the end of the road and their was a forest in front of us. "We have to walk from here."

"If you say so," I replied. We got out of the car and started into the tropical forest. It was really warm and humid. "Now what," I asked.

"Follow the path," she told me.

"What path," I asked, "I don't see a path." She bent down and spread the plants apart to reveal mud and in the mud were footprints. We followed the path of footprints.

Meanwhile, David was walking with Calandra and a few of his followers. They sat down to take a break. One of his followers was carrying our equipment and put the bag down. After about five minutes they got up and started walking. They didn't realize that our equipment was left laying in the bushes nearby.

Heather and I saw that we got to a place where they rested. "They rested here," Heather told me, "and my dream is trying to tell me something." She sat down and concentrated. "I see our time belts," she told me, "our equipment, it's near." I started looking around. Then I saw it. I screamed out in joy.

"Now they're in trouble," I told Heather, "we are officially the Time Warriors."

"Let's go," she said, "they're not far." We loaded up our belts with equipment. We continued to walk through the woods.

"What now," I asked her.

"I don't know," she said, "my dreams died down. I'm not getting signals." Just then she screamed out in pain.

"What," I asked in fear, "what's going on?"

"I don't know," she replied, "it's like someone is in my head and messing up my thoughts."

"How are we supposed to find them if your thoughts are messed up," I asked. Just then there was an explosion and a wave of wind flew past us. I looked around in shock. Then I saw, in the distance, streams of energy falling to the ground. I knew it was them.

"That's them," she said, "but I am in too much pain to go."

"We have to," I told her, "it's our only chance."

"Just go," she told me. I ran toward the energy lights. When I came into the clearing, there was a huge temple and the energy beams were entering it. I ran toward the temple but as I went to step on the steps to go in, a wave of wind blew me backwards into a tree. Then the ground started rumbling. Heather ran up to me.

"It's them," she told me, "they are trying to stop us from getting in."

"They're doing a good job," I told her.

"Use the time belts to warp," she told me. We did exactly that and the next thing I knew we were in the temple. There were five huge statues of fairy-like creatures. One in each corner and one in the middle of the room. I walked around.

"Terra," I told her. Just then the ground started to shake. We looked around and from the ground came warriors. We started fighting the warriors. I punched one but it threw me backwards.

"It's no use," Heather told me, "they are too strong." We ran down a hallway and heard voices. But then there was a strange sound and then we saw water coming down the hallway toward us.

"Run," I told her. We started running back toward the room we were in. The wave of water washed us away and we gasped for air whenever we got a chance. The water carried us out of the temple and we fell on our backs on the ground. Then David, Calandra, and a lady I had never seen before were standing on the steps in front of us.

"Mommy," Calandra screamed. I climbed to my feet and started running toward them. The lady lifter her hands in the air and pushed them forward. A gust of wind hit me and pushed me backwards. Heather ran toward them and suddenly fell to her knees, screaming in pain. David laughed.

"Time Warriors leaders," he said, "I want you to meet my backup and new best friend. Her name is Karma and she has the four crystals of the elements and has their powers. She also, herself, has the power to control minds with psychic energy. That is what is happening to Heather. That is who has been causing Heather to have the dreams. Now it is time for you two to make a decision. Karma is going to use her powers to destroy the world. Calandra and I are going to take a trip in time. Who are you going to concentrate on?" He picked Calandra up and hit his time belt and they were gone. I looked at Heather and then at Karma. She laughed and disappeared into the temple. Heather got up and looked at me.

"World or daughter," Heather said as she looked at me.

"Time travel it is," I told her and she smiled. "The other four will take care of Karma." We hit our time belts and entered the warp zone. Little did David know but we had a tracking device on all the time belts so we were able to follow him into time.

CHAPTER THIRTEEN

Meanwhile, the other four warriors were on the quest to find the temples. They were sitting in our headquarters. "Ok," Chris said, "I'll take the Temple of Fire in Hawaii. Krissy, I want you to go to the Temple of Wind in Germany. Steph, you take the Temple of Water in the depths of the Atlantic Ocean. William, you take the Temple of Earth in Africa. We will all meet back here before we head to South America for the Temple of Life. By that time, Heather and TJ should have Calandra and be battling there in South America." The other three agreed and they split up.

Heather and I arrived somewhere in the future and immediately I started exploring for clues. I turned around and got hit in the face by David. Heather ran toward him but got cut off by one of his followers. The city that we were in seemed to be very advanced. David grabbed Calandra from the woman that was holding her and started running through the city. Heather and I followed pushing our way through the crowd. Then I saw a sign that told me we were in New York City. David ran to a dock of some sort and got on a floating balloon-like device with Calandra. It started to rise into the air. Heather and I got to the dock and shot our slingshots at the device. It pulled us up with it. David put Calandra down and started to kick at the ropes we were hanging on. We were swinging back and forth rapidly.

"Hold on," I told Heather. She looked at me in fear. We were still over concrete and would never survive the fall.

"Do something," she told me, "I want our daughter back." I started thinking of various things I could do. We were now over the ocean and could survive a fall to the water. I grabbed the knife off my belt. Heather looked at me.

"Hold on," I told her, "we're going for a ride." I threw the knife at the balloon and it popped. The device started falling toward the water.

"Get Calandra," Heather screamed, "she'll never make it to the surface." We hit the water and I dove down with the impact. I was searching through the water for Calandra. Heather was doing the same. I pulled my water-proof flashlight out and it lit up the water. Then I saw Calandra and I started swimming toward her. I went to grab her hand but she disappeared. I couldn't hold my breath any longer so I shot toward the surface. Heather looked at me.

"I almost had her but she disappeared," I told Heather.

"What do you mean she disappeared," Heather asked. "She can't just disappear." Then I thought about it. She had some kind of bracelet on her arm.

"David put a time bracelet on her wrist," I replied, "when he warped, so did she."

"Shit," Heather cried, "we were this close."

"We still are," I told her. I hit my time belt and was in the warp zone. Heather followed my lead. I saw David and Calandra flying through the tunnel in front of me. I clicked my boots to get my rocket boosters. Heather did the same and we caught up to David. I punched David as I collided into him. He let go of Calandra with the impact and Heather grabbed her in her arms. David pulled out a gun of some sort and shot time energy at us. It pushed us back and with the impact knocked Calandra out of Heather's arm.

"Get the bracelet off of her," I told Heather, "or else he can still take her with him." Heather grabbed for Calandra's arm but the time energy pushed us backward and David and Calandra disappeared.

"Noooo," Heather screamed. She tried to push forward but the time energy was too strong. It wouldn't let up.

"We have to break past this time energy," I told Heather, "or it is going to take us out of the warp zone."

"Then what happens," Heather asked as we tried to resist being pushed backwards.

"We die," I responded. I clicked my boots together again to add more power to the rocket boosters but it didn't help. Then I saw the end of the warp zone.

"That's not good," Heather cried.

"No it's not," I replied. I pulled out my laser and shot it at the energy bubble. Heather did the same.

"It's not working," Heather screamed.

"Hit your time belt," I told her. We both pressed our time belts and warped out of the bubble into the warp zone.

"That was close," she sighed in relief.

"We're not safe yet," I told her, "if that hits the end of the warp zone, the energy is going to come back and kill us."

"What is it with death and us," Heather screamed. We clicked our boots together and the rocket boosters pushed us away from the end and toward the Earth. The bubble hit the end and the energy spread throughout the warp zone and headed toward us. We fell into Earth right as the energy came past. We were safe, but our daughter was not.

CHAPTER FOURTEEN

William stood looking down into the tunnel that would take him into the Temple of Earth. "They want me to go in their by myself," he said, "yeah right." Just then a little boy ran up to him.

"You're a Time Warrior," the little boy exclaimed, "my heroes. Go get the bad guys!" He started doing karate moves on the air. William laughed and nodded at the little boy.

"Ok," William told himself, "here goes nothing. Be a hero!" He walked down the steps and into the tunnel. He pulled out his flashlight and looked around. He stood outside the door to the temple and looked up. The sign read 'Temple of Earth: Home of the Element Terra.' He started talking to himself again, "as Chris would say, let's kick some elemental ass." He walked through the door and slowly and cautiously looked around. He walked through the first room and into the second. He crossed the thin narrow bridge and made his way through the rest of the temple. When he entered the main chamber he saw the altar and that the crystal was missing. "What do I need," he asked himself, "the crystal is gone. I really should have paid attention to the story."

The ground started to shake. "That's not good," he said. Then four Terra Warriors popped out of the ground. "Really not good." He punched one in the face and kicked another in the stomach. One pushed him into the wall and he ducked as it swung at him. "How do I beat the Terra Warriors," he pondered, "the old lady didn't tell us this." Just then a cool breeze came over the temple and he heard a whisper.

"Find the spirit of earth within you young warrior," the whisper said, "the spirit of earth is in you." He shrugged his shoulders.

"What is that supposed to mean." Then he saw a boulder sitting in the corner of the room. "I got it," use earth to beat earth." He grabbed the boulder and threw it at the warriors. They fell down. Then he pushed another boulder out of the corner to reveal a hole in the floor. He stood by the hole. "Hey, stupid Terra Warriors," he yelled. They ran toward him. He fell on his back in front of the hole and used his legs to push them over his body and into the hole. They fell out of sight. "Hah," he said cockily, "I'm a true warrior." Just then something hit him from behind and he barely jumped over the hole.

"What the hell," he cried as he turned around. There was a Terra Warrior standing in front of him only more muscular than the other ones. It had a green necklace on its neck. "That's it," he said, "I need the necklace." The warrior knocked him down on his back. He hit his head on the rocky floor and rubbed it. "This is not going to be fun," he assured himself. The warrior walked toward him and he kicked it in the stomach but he only hurt his foot. "Too strong, not smart," William surveyed the situation. "I have to outsmart him." He grabbed his long shot and jumped down the hole. As he was falling he shot the long shot up and it grabbed onto the edge of the hole. He stopped and swung back and forth. The warrior jumped down and grabbed onto him. William pulled the necklace off the warrior and kicked him in the ribs. The warrior held onto the rope and William climbed up. As soon as he reached the top he grabbed onto the edge of the hole and pulled the long shot out and the warrior fell. William climbed out and put the necklace around his neck. Shivers went up and down his body. He ran out of the temple and warped back to headquarters.

CHAPTER FIFTEEN

Heather and I stood where we landed trying to figure out where we were now. There was some kind of a festival going on in the streets around us. "What's going on," Heather asked.

"I don't know," I answered. I tried to pick out some tradition that would tell me which festival this was. I could tell we were in the past instead of the future. It was country-western music playing so I figured we were somewhere either south or west of home. There were people dancing around and singing. Heather walked up to a girl dancing. The girl was probably about seventeen and had blonde hair. She seemed to be the center of attention of a group of guys.

"Excuse me," Heather interrupted, "excuse me." They ignored her. "EXCUSE ME!!!!" The girl continued to dance but some of the guys took their attention to Heather. "What is this festival," Heather asked.

"This festival celebrates the birth of our country," the one guy said.

"Is it the fourth of July," Heather asked.

"Yeah," he said, "and here in Nashville we celebrate it like this. You dance the entire night. Then later we have fireworks." Heather came back over to me and explained all of that to me.

"Why would David come here," I asked. "What would he want here?"

"He's trying to tell us something," Heather replied. "The question is, what?" We walked around the festival looking for David and Calandra. As we were walking a guy came up and grabbed Heather and pulled her over to a group of his friends. They were trying to get her to dance. I looked over and started to walk toward them.

"Daddy," Calandra screamed. I looked over and saw David pushing his way through the crowd with Calandra.

"Heather," I screamed, "let's go." She looked at me and tried to walk away from the group but they stopped her. The one guy grabbed her around her waist and she punched him in the stomach. She pushed past him and ran over to me. We pushed through the crowd after David. David hopped on a horse nearby and road away. Heather and I hopped on two other horses that were there and followed him. The fireworks started going off behind us. Just then we heard the crowd scream. Heather and I stopped our horses and turned around to see a firework flying toward the crowd and then there was a flash. After that all we saw was a massive pile of bodies on the ground.

"I think I got the point he is trying to prove," I told Heather.

"So do I," she responded. We turned around to find David and Calandra leaving. We hit our time belts and followed them through the warp zone.

Meanwhile, back in the present, in Washington, Johnson was watching television when the President was about to make an emergency announcement. The President walked onto the stand. "We need to have a city lockdown. Ladies and gentlemen, this is not because of a threat, it is just a precaution. The Time Warriors are busy investigating a mission, which could pose a threat to us so we need to be careful. Please go on with your everyday lives but be cautious. Look for people carrying weird necklaces and crystals. If you should see these suspicious things please call the D.C. police and tell them what you are witnessing. The Time Warriors have always protected us before and I know they will this time but be cautious. This time it is a lot more powerful of a force. As always, be careful and live free. Good night and God bless."

CHAPTER SIXTEEN

"I got the necklace," William told the others through the watch communicators.

"I'm about to go in," Steph radioed back.

Meanwhile, Heather and I landed in an unknown time of the future. "Now what," she asked me. "Where are we?"

"The real question," I told her, "is what is our next obstacle?" Just then a dart hit Heather in the right shoulder. I looked around but saw nothing. I pulled the dart out of her shoulder. A force field surrounded me and I tried to break free. Another dart hit her shoulder and she fell over. I used my belt to warp out of the force field and ran to her. A wave of energy hit me and I flew backwards. I looked to see a group of guys in black outfits made out of metal pick Heather up. I ran toward them but they disappeared before I could reach them.

"What do they want with her," I asked myself out loud.

"She is sentenced to death," a voice said. I looked to see a girl, about nineteen years old standing nearby.

"Why would they sentence her to death," I asked her.

"She is over the age of eighteen. I am over eighteen as well. See they were looking for me, but they got her instead," the girl explained. "I'm Angela," she told me as she shook my hand.

"I'm TJ," I told her. "Why would they sentence you to death?"

"The men that run the government feel that it was women that caused the Earth to be destroyed," she explained.

"This isn't Earth," I asked with confusion.

"This is Mars sweetie," she continued, "and so any girl over eighteen is sentenced to death. In fact, they stopped creating females a few years ago. Now, all babies are males."

"How do they keep the population without women?"

"They have artificial ways."

"Why would men want to get rid of women," I said questioning the logic, "that doesn't make sense."

"Well," she said, "they created computer generated women to serve them. They say they listen better than real women."

"What a weird world," I said. "But I can't talk, I have to get her back real quick."

"I wouldn't suggest that," she replied, "they will kill you."

"I have to," I continued, "she is my wife and the mother of my child." Angela gasped in horror. "What?"

"Don't let them find that out," she told me, "you will be tortured for sinning."

"Sinning," I asked. "How is that sinning?"

"Being married to and having a child with a real woman," she said quietly, "is the worst thing a man can do." I shook my head in disbelief.

"I heard enough," I told her. "How do I get to her?"

"They are taking her to their lab, where they will do tests on her. Then she will be sent to court and they will decide her fate. Either she will be imprisoned and used for artificial creation and be a slave worker, or she will be sentenced to death."

"How do I get there," I asked.

"This will be dangerous," she told me, "but I will help you."

"You will," I questioned her with surprise.

"Yeah," she answered, "after all it isn't like I have a chance to get this close to a guy again. The men live in villages and we aren't allowed near them. This is the first time I have seen a real man instead of one of those soldier-bred freaks." I couldn't believe what I was hearing. I looked to the sky and saw the glass that kept the oxygen in the atmosphere.

"I am happily married," I told her, "so don't get any ideas."

"Don't worry," she told me, "those of us women that are here are programmed so that we don't have the emotion of love or attraction in us."

"If this is where our civilization is headed," I said, "I am glad I'm living now."

"You're a time traveler aren't you?"

"Yeah."

"Are you one of the warriors in the legend?"

"Yeah, I guess."

"Time traveling is eventually banned."

"I would love to talk, but I have to find my wife so we can find our daughter. We really have to hurry."

"Right," she responded, "you first." She pointed which way to go.

"Ok," I said as I started walking in the direction she told me.

"Stay in the shadows," she told me.

"Talk about women's rights," I said, "the feminists would not like this idea." Then we heard voices coming down the alley we were in.

"We have to hide," she cried. I looked around as she was screaming in fear. I heard footsteps running toward us. I grabbed her arm and pulled her behind some boxes and crates. I held her still because she was freaking out. The soldiers ran past us and we stood up. The light above us allowed me to see what she looked like. She was very pretty and had brown hair.

"We all are," she told me, "that's why they kept us."

"You all are what," I questioned her.

"Don't try to fool me," she said, "I know what you are thinking. You're a guy and even though I haven't been around any, I still know their instincts." I laughed at her prediction of men. "I can't be attracted," she told herself, "I am programmed not to be." I looked at her trying to understand what she was doing. She pushed me along and we started walking again.

"What a strange society," I told her, but she was ignoring me. She was too wrapped up in thought.

"Are you ok," I asked. She was still rambling to herself and I had no idea what she was talking about.

"Are you alright," I asked again.

"Yeah," she finally answered, "just trying to figure a way in."

"In where," I asked. She was in the thought process again. She wasn't paying attention. I wasn't even sure if we were going the right way anymore.

"In my friend's building," she responded.

"I thought we were going to the lab," I said, "where my wife is."

"We are," she answered, "but I'm going to get my friend Kelsi to come with us." I was confused. I looked up and saw cameras on the buildings.

"We might be followed," I told her, "there are cameras watching us."

"We're here," she said as she opened the door and walked in. We went up the steps to an apartment on the second floor. She knocked on the door and waited.

"Who is it," a girl answered.

"Kelsi," Angela said, "it's me, Angela." The door opened to reveal another pretty girl with blonde hair. Kelsi saw me and slammed the door.

"Oh no," she yelled from the other side of the door, "you are not bringing a guy into my apartment. I am not getting caught."

"Come on," Angela yelled back, "he is the time traveler, the warrior in the legend. He needs our help and in return he will help us." She looked at me.

"Exactly," I replied hesitantly. Kelsi opened the door for us to come in. I went in and sat down on the couch.

"I am attracted to this guy," Angela told Kelsi in the kitchen. "I know I'm not supposed to be, but look at him. It is my instinct breaking through all the conditioning. But we have to help him save his wife and daughter." Kelsi gasped in shock at that statement. "I know what the law is, but he is not from our time and his wife is captured. Plus it will take us a few days to get to the lab. Think about the time we will get to spend with this guy. It sounds so weird to say it."

"Think about the danger," Kelsi replied. "What if we get caught?" Just then the door flew open and soldiers ran in. I jumped off the couch and kicked one. I ran into the kitchen. The girls screamed when they saw the soldiers. I punched another one and kicked another as they came in the kitchen.

"Go," I told the girls. They jumped out the kitchen window and fell into boxes below. I followed after them. We ran down the alley. I ran ahead of them and opened a sewer drain. I grabbed Angela and lowered her down into the sewer and then did the same with Kelsi. I jumped in and closed the sewer drain.

"Keep quiet," I told them. I could hear the soldiers running down the alley above. The sound disappeared and I relaxed, trying to catch my breath.

"I guess I have no choice now," Kelsi said.

"I guess not," I told her. "Stay here, I am going to walk down this tunnel and see where it leads." I walked away.

The girls laughed and I wondered what they were up to.

"What," I asked.

"So your wife is captured and you have a daughter," Kelsi asked.

"Yeah," I answered, "and my wife is pregnant again."

"What," Angela asked in fear.

"She's pregnant with our second," I replied. Before I could finish, Kelsi butted in.

"They'll kill here immediately if they find that out," Kelsi said.

"Or at least the baby," Angela added.

"Then we really have to hurry," I urged them.

CHAPTER SEVENTEEN

Meanwhile, in the present, the rest of the team had captured their necklaces and were preparing to battle with Karma.

"I'm hungry," Angela said. It was dusk and we were preparing to head for the lab.

"Me too," Kelsi added.

"Can you go up there and get us some food," Angela asked me.

"I suppose," I replied. I cautiously climbed out of the sewer and got some weird looking pizza and solar juice from a nearby stand. I took it down to the girls and they dug in.

"Aren't you going to eat," Kelsi asked.

"I think I'll pass," I told her. Angela couldn't open he solar juice so she gave it to me. I pulled it open and it splashed on my shirt.

"Wash it out now," Kelsi said, "it will stain."

"Over there," Angela pointed to clean water running out of a pipe. I took off my shirt and walked over to the pipe and scrubbed the juice out.

"Hot," Kelsi told Angela.

"The pizza," they said together, "it's really hot." I looked back at what I was doing. They smiled at each other behind my back.

"Are you two coming," I asked.

"Oh," Kelsi said. They followed me toward the sewer drain. I put my shirt on as I was walking, even though it was still wet. We climbed out of the sewer when I saw that it was safe.

"There's the lab," Kelsi pointed high up on a hill.

"What about your daughter," Angela asked.

"They left this time," I answered. "I'm outta here as soon as I get Heather."

"Heather," Kelsi questioned, "is that your wife's name?" I nodded my head and started walking toward the hill.

"We'll see what is so special about this Heather," Angela told Kelsi. I got on a motorcycle that was sitting against a building.

"What are you doing," Kelsi asked.

"Getting to the lab a little quicker," I answered.

"You can't steal the cycle," Angela told me.

"I'm not stealing," I replied, "I'm borrowing."

"Ok, but," Kelsi started.

"Get on," I cut in.

"But," Angela cried.

"Now," I ordered, "or stay here." Kelsi got on behind me and

Angela behind her. "Hang on," I told them as I started the bike. Kelsi wrapped her arms tightly around me.

"No problem," Kelsi said joyfully. Angela held on to the back of Kelsi. I drove off toward the lab.

We got to the hill and we got off the bike. I decided we would climb the hill by foot because we would be less likely to get caught. We began our climb and then I saw soldiers running toward us.

"Run," I screamed to the girls. They took off in opposite directions. The guards hit Angela with darts and she collapsed. Moments later, I could not find Angela or Kelsi. A guard came walking toward me.

"You were with women," he said to me, "you shall be sentenced to death." I punched him and then kneed him in the stomach. He pushed me backwards and I fell and hit my head on a rock. He came walking towards me and I kicked him backwards. A dart hit me in the shoulder and I quickly pulled it out. The guard came running at me and I stabbed him in the shoulder with the dart. He fell over and was motionless.

"I could use his uniform to get inside the lab," I told myself. I took his uniform off him and found that it was actually a robot. I took my outfit off and started putting the robot uniform on. Kelsi came back and smiled when she saw I wasn't completely dressed. I quickly finished putting the uniform on. I realized it wouldn't be easy to move in the metal suit.

"So this is how they are bred," she said as she looked at the robot.

"Yeah," I told her, "they aren't even real men, that is why they have no interest in you."

"I saw you were human though," she said as she smiled at me.

"Enough," I exclaimed, "we have to get inside." I started walking up the hill again.

"I can't go in like this," she yelled to me. I saw a guard so I bashed its head in with a rock and took his uniform.

"Here," I told Kelsi, "put this on." She took the outfit out of my hands and started getting undressed. I turned away and waited for her to finish.

"What am I supposed to do with my hair," she questioned. I took the helmet that the guard was wearing and pushed her hair up and put the helmet one her head. Then I took some of the pieces that the robot had on its face and put is on her face to hide that she was a girl.

"There," I said, "that's the best I can do." She kissed me without warning but I pushed away.

"Now what," she asked, "I know you wanted me to do that."

"You look like a man," I replied with disgust.

"In this case I'll take that as a compliment."

"I mean I'm married. I love Heather."

"I think you're questioning yourself." I walked away and found a pipe in the ground.

"This is our way in," I told her. We slid down the pipe and made our way through a dark hallway. I walked up to the first soldier I saw.

"We have been ordered to check on recently capture women," I explained. He let us in and I saw Heather in a prison cell.

"Her," Kelsi said with a deep voice, "that is the one we need." She was talking about Angela. The guard opened the cell and Kelsi took Angela out.

"That one too," I told the guard pointing to Heather. He let her out. I grabbed Heather by the arm and started walking out of the building. Kelsi and Angela were behind us. Angela and Heather had no idea that it was us because of the metal covering our faces. Heather kept trying to get away, but I held on to her. When we got outside the building, the guards we attacked were there.

"Run," Kelsi screamed. We started running down the hill.

"What are you doing," Heather cried still not knowing it was me. "Let go!" We continued down the hill. On the way down I grabbed my time belt that was laying with my uniform. I unhooked Heather's belt from her waist.

"Hurry," Kelsi cried as they were catching up to us.

"Don't touch me," Heather screamed as she tried to push my hands away. I threw my belt to Kelsi.

"On three push the button," I told her. "One, two, three." We both pushed the buttons. I held tightly onto Heather and resisted against her kicking and screaming. We entered the warp zone and before we knew it, we were back in the present.

CHAPTER EIGHTEEN

"**W**ho the hell do you think you are," Heather asked. I took the helmet off and pulled the metal off my face. "Oh my God," she exclaimed as she hugged and kissed me. Kelsi took her helmet off and Angela was shocked.

"This is Kelsi and Angela," I told Heather. "And this is Heather," I introduced her to Kelsi and Angela. "Angela and Kelsi helped me find you, so I decided to get them out of their fate."

"How did you pull this off," Heather cried still holding and kissing me.

"I was lucky," I told her.

"It was more than that," Kelsi said, "he is good."

"Now we have to find Calandra," I told them.

"Is that your daughter," Angela asked.

"Yeah," I answered.

"Where do you think they went," Heather asked.

"Did you have any more dreams," I questioned her.

"Yeah," she replied, "something about our team wearing necklaces. And Calandra was with our team."

Meanwhile, our team met in Argentina at the Temple of Life. "Now that we have the necklaces we shouldn't have a problem," Chris said.

"Now what do we do," Krissy asked.

"Wait for TJ and Heather," Chris told her, "because Heather is the one with the dreams."

"I say we head for a hotel," William added.

"Good idea," Chris replied.

In D.C., I was showing Kelsi and Angela the offices at our headquarters. "Can I get you some sandwiches," Heather asked us. We all nodded.

"I'll help you," Angela said as she walked toward the hall where Heather was standing. They disappeared down the hall. I sat down on the edge of my desk.

"So this is your team," Kelsi said as she examined a picture on my wall.

"Yeah," I answered.

"Where are the other four members now?"

"Saving the world somewhere," I replied.

"Who are they," she asked looking at the picture.

"Well this is my best friend Chris," I started while pointing at the picture. "That is his girlfriend, Steph. That's my cousin Krissy and her boyfriend William."

"What's a girlfriend," Kelsi asked.

"A boyfriend or girlfriend is when you just met and are going out to find out if you love each other. If you find out that you want to spend the rest of your life together, you get engaged and become fiancées. Then you have a ceremony and get married to be husband and wife.

"I think I understand," she said. "So I could be your girlfriend and you wouldn't be committed to me, you would be committed to Heather."

"No," I told her, "because I am married, I can't have a girlfriend or fiancée."

Meanwhile, the team was walking toward the steps of the hotel. "That's the Time Warriors," David screamed. He pushed Calandra to them and backed away. "We don't need her now," he told them. "We want to let you concentrate on trying to beat us. We want a challenge." He hit the warp button with his group and they disappeared. Steph looked over Calandra to make sure she was ok.

"I have to get changed into another warrior outfit," I told Kelsi, "stay here." I walked to the elevator and pushed the button. When the door opened, Heather and Angela walked off carrying sandwiches.

"I'm going to get changed," I told them. "I'll be right back."

"Ok," Heather replied. Heather led Angela into my office to meet Kelsi. "So how old are you," she asked them.

"Nineteen," they responded.

"How come you weren't caught," Heather continued.

"They didn't find us," Kelsi admitted.

"So you have never seen a guy before TJ," Heather questioned, "except the robotic soldiers."

"Right," Angela said.

"But you are conditioned so that you can't love or be attracted to guys," Heather pointed out. "Right?"

"Right," Kelsi responded.

"Good," Heather sighed with relief, "then I have nothing to worry about." I walked in and caught the end of the conversation.

"What's up," I asked.

"Let's make these two new members of the team," Heather told me.

"Great idea," Kelsi exclaimed with joy.

"Awesome," Angela added.

"I don't think that's a good idea," I complained knowing how Kelsi was acting toward me.

"Come on," Heather pleaded, "you'll need someone to take my

place when I'm out with the baby. You are going to keep working, aren't you? That's what you told me."

"Yeah," Kelsi added, "I can take her place."

"I am going to keep working," I replied, "but I don't think it's a good idea."

"It's a great idea," Heather cut in. "I didn't like Steph joining the team because she originally had a crush on you, but it turned out to work. This time, I don't have to worry about that."

"Exactly," Kelsi said with an evil smile.

"Please," Heather begged, "I will feel better while I'm out knowing that you have a partner."

"What can I do," Angela asked.

"We'll figure something out," Heather assured her.

"Fine," I reluctantly accepted.

"I'll tell Johnson to make them outfits," Heather said and she was really pleased. She kissed me on the way out. I walked over to the snack room to get a soda.

"Did you hear that," Kelsi asked Angela, "I can take her place." I got the soda and started walking back when my watch beeped.

"This is TJ," I said into it.

"It's Chris," the voice replied, "we have Calandra."

"Are you serious," I exclaimed, "that's great."

"But you better get down here," he continued, "the battle is going to begin. We're in Argentina at the Temple of Life."

"Right away," I replied. I ran down the steps to Johnson's lab. Heather was talking with Johnson about making outfits.

"What," she asked.

"They got Calandra," I explained, "she's ok."

"Who," Heather questioned.

"The team, they have her."

"Oh, awesome, that's great."

"We have to go now, the battle is going to begin."

"Good luck," Johnson said as we ran out and up the steps to my office.

"Stay here," I told Kelsi and Angela, "Johnson will get you set up. We have to go." Before they could say anything, Heather and I were in the warp zone. I locked our tracking device on the other members' belts.

CHAPTER NINETEEN

The other members of the team stood outside the Temple of Life with Calandra. "I thought they were coming," Krissy said.

"They are," Chris told her, "give them time." Just then there was an explosion from inside the temple and waves of energy were shooting toward the sky.

"I don't think we have time," William cried.

"Patience is a virtue," Steph told him.

"Not when the force of a million bombs is about to be unleashed on the planet," Chris replied. "We can't wait for them, we have to act now."

"We need our leaders," Krissy begged, "so wait."

"We can't," William pleaded with fear in his voice. "There isn't time. Plus Chris and Steph can lead the team as good as, if not better, than Heather and TJ."

"Thank you," Chris and Steph replied together.

"No problem," William continued.

"Liar," Krissy mumbled under her breath. The energy waves were getting bigger.

"It's Karma," Steph cried.

"Move in," Chris ordered. Chris grabbed Calandra and they ran up the steps into the temple. Chris looked around cautiously.

"Remember," Steph said, "we have the same powers she does." Steph suddenly collapsed to her knees in pain.

"What," Chris asked with fear in his voice.

"She's in my head," Steph screamed in pain."

"Who," William asked.

"Karma," Steph continued with tears in her eyes.

"She's trying to get to us," Chris told them, "don't let her win."

"Mommy," Calandra muttered.

"That's right," Chris said, "Karma did this to your mommy."

"They trapped TJ and Heather in the warp zone," Steph explained, "I can see it in my head." Just then David's gang ran in. Krissy grabbed Calandra and put her behind one of the statues, a statue of Terra.

"Stay here," Krissy ordered her. Krissy ran back to the rest of the team. The gang attacked the team. Chris and William were fighting the gang off, but Krissy fell to her knees in pain like Steph. One of the gang members pushed William backwards. William hit his head and laid motionless on the floor.

"Great," Chris cried, "I could really use some help." The gang surrounded Chris. Meanwhile, behind the statue, Calandra saw a button.

"Fine," Chris yelled, "you play with fire, you're going to get burnt." He went to use the power of the necklace but Calandra pressed the button and the temple started shaking. The gang ran out of the temple in fear.

"What did you do," Chris asked Calandra with fear and frustration.

"Button," she mumbled.

"Why do you have to take after Krissy," Chris pleaded with her, "and touch everything?" The statue's eyes blinked.

"Statue alive," Calandra said with a giggle.

"No," Chris replied, "you are seeing things." Then one of the statue's arms moved. "I have to use my phrase," Chris continued, "das ist nicht so gut." The statue walked toward him. Chris kicked it but only hurt his foot because it was solid rock. Then the other three statues moved toward him.

"I'll use my other saying now," Chris said, "oh shit."

"Shit," Calandra replied.

"Yes," Chris told her, "that is what you say in a situation like this." The four statues, all made of solid rock were now surrounding Chris. Chris grabbed the necklace and concentrated hard on it. A wave of fire shot out and the statue of Aqua was destroyed.

"That's it," he exclaimed, "each crystal destroys a different statue. Fire evaporates water. Now I need the water crystal from Steph to extinguish fire over here." He ran over to Steph, who was still crying in pain on the floor and took the crystal. He concentrated on it and nothing happened.

"Master power," Calandra said.

"That's right," Chris replied, "you have to beat the element to get the power. Steph has to use this necklace." He gave it back to Steph. "Concentrate on this," he demanded.

"I can't," she cried. The statues came toward him slowly. Just then a wave of earth flew through and the statue of Aer was destroyed. William was standing there with the necklace in his hand.

The statue of Ignis and Terra continued toward him. A gust of wind swept through the room and destroyed the statue of Terra. Krissy overcame the pain in her head and was standing with the necklace raised in front of her. Finally Steph shot water and destroyed Ignis. Chris was relieved and then he looked at Calandra.

"Don't touch anything," he told her. Calandra sat down and played with a stone on the floor.

"We're ok," Steph said. "We overcame her power."

"That's what you think," a voice said from behind them. They turned around and saw that Karma and David had entered the room. "You forgot about my statue," Karma continued. She clapped her hands and the statue woke up and punched a hole in the wall.

"Not good," Steph cried.

"Really not good," Krissy replied.

"Only one of your teammates knows how to beat this one," Karma explained, "and she is stuck in the warp zone."

"Heather," Chris yelled. Karma laughed evilly with that being said.

"Oh shit," Calandra said and she laughed. Steph looked at Chris with an evil eye and he shrugged his shoulders.

Meanwhile, in the warp zone, Heather and I were trying to figure out how to get out. "They put some kind of force field over the warp zone," I said.

"Then put a warp zone over a warp zone," Heather told me, "rewarp." We did exactly that and it worked.

Back at the Temple of Life, the statue chased William and Chris down a dark hallway. Steph ran at Karma but Karma shot a geyser of water at Steph. The force of the water pushed Steph backwards into the wall. Krissy shot a gust of wind at Karma, but it was blocked when Karma created a mini-mountain in front of her. Then she shot a gust of wind at Krissy and Krissy was thrown backwards into the wall. Karma laughed with her trademark evil laugh. William, Chris, and the statue reentered the room.

"Help," Chris screamed. Heather and I appeared and assessed the battle. "Heather," Chris said, "you know how to defeat this statue."

Heather looked at me and I shrugged my shoulders. The statue picked William up and threw him across the room, then it did the same thing to Chris.

"Hurry," I told Heather. Heather closed her eyes and searched through her memories. The statue picked me up and I tried to get fee.

"I got it," Heather yelled, "use all of the powers together." The four team members did exactly that. The statue threw me against the wall and I hit the floor with a thud. But seconds later, the statue was nothing but a pile of rocks.

CHAPTER TWENTY

"Looks like you're finished Karma," Krissy exclaimed. Karma laughed at that comment.

"I'm only beginning," she replied, "without Heather, your team is nothing."

"I'm not going anywhere," Heather told her. Karma looked at Calandra. Heather ran and grabbed her, knowing that Karma was going to do something.

"David," Karma said, "now."

"Heather," I screamed from where I was, still holding my head from hitting the wall, "the bracelet!"

"Oh my God," she cried as she tried to get the bracelet off. David hit the warp button and he disappeared. Then Calandra disappeared right out of Heather's arms. Karma laughed evilly again and Heather became furious. She looked at Karma and then at me.

"No," I screamed to her. She ran at Karma. Karma shot wind at her, but Heather avoided it. Then Karma shot a geyser of water at her, but she avoided that as well. She got to Karma and kicked her. Karma stumbled backwards and stood against the wall. Karma shot fire at Heather but Steph used water to put it out. Karma punched the wall and the temple began to crack. Heather jumped around the cracks in the floor and punched Karma again. Karma shot wind but William protected Heather with mini-mountains. Heather jumped over one and kicked Karma in the face. Karma shot a geyser of water but Chris evaporated it before it hit Heather.

"You thought I would chase after my daughter," Heather cried in anger, "I will, after I kill you." Karma laughed as she shot dirt at Heather to blind her. Krissy used wind gusts to blow the dirt back in Karma's face. Heather took the opportunity to get punches and kicks in on Karma. Karma fell to the ground and then shot psychic beams at Heather. Heather fell to the ground in pain.

"You forgot," Karma said, "I control your mind."

"Fight it," I told Heather as she cried in agony.

"Do something," Steph begged me.

"I can't," I replied, "she has to overcome this herself." Heather struggled to her feet.

"Shoot me with each of your powers," Heather told the rest of the team.

"What," Chris questioned, "won't it kill you?"

"Do it," Heather yelled. The team looked at me for permission. I didn't know what to say.

"You're the leader," Steph said, "you make the call." I looked at Heather, her eyes begging me to tell them to do it. The team stared at me, waiting for the order.

"Do it," I responded as I nodded my head. They all shot their powers at Heather.

"This is going to be like a nuclear bomb," Chris warned.

"Keep going," Heather cried in pain. The powers were too much for her and she fell to her knees on the ground.

"It's going to kill her," Steph told me.

"Don't stop," Heather begged.

"Stop," I yelled.

"Not yet," Heather pleaded. The team looked at me in confusion.

"Keep going," I told them. Karma was laughing. Heather fell over and became unconscious. "Stop," I yelled. They cut the power and we stood, watching in horror as Heather just laid there.

"You fools," Karma laughed, "you killed her. And now you won't be able to defeat me." Just then Heather moved. She started to climb slowly to her feet. When she was completely standing, she looked into Karma's eyes.

"What goes around," Heather said, "comes around Karma." Karma stared at her in surprise. Heather opened her arms and a ball of energy, containing all four elements, was created.

"What," Karma cried in fear.

"I'm using your mind power with their powers to destroy you," Heather explained. Karma backed up in fear as I crossed my fingers. Heather threw the ball of energy at Karma. It hit her and she flew backwards through the wall. Heather walked into the next room where she was laying.

"Is she dead," I asked.

"She will be shortly," Heather told me.

"Now to get David," I replied.

"Head back to D.C.," Heather told the rest of the team. "This is our job." We hit the warp buttons and disappeared.

When we landed in the time where David was, he was already battling with Kelsi and Angela. Heather ran to Calandra and ripped the bracelet off her wrist. Kelsi and Angela grabbed David's arms and disappeared into the warp zone.

"Where are they going," Heather asked.

"I don't know," I said, "but maybe we should follow."

"No," she told me, "they are our team now, et them take care of it. Let's go home and get Calandra settled."

When we got back to our house, the other four were waiting for us. Then Kelsi and Angela appeared.

"What did you do with David," I asked.

"We locked him up in a time when men were banned," Kelsi said. "Revenge on men."

"Who are they," Chris asked.

"The two newest members to our team," Heather replied, "Kelsi and Angela."

"Kelsi is going to be my partner while Heather is out on maternity leave," I told them.

"Let's get some sleep," Heather said. Heather and I put Calandra in her room. Kelsi and Angela stayed downstairs and the others went home. Heather and I laid down.

"Are you ok with me working while you are out," I asked.

"As long as you work with Kelsi," she answered. "You need a partner."

"No one could take your place," I told her, " you were awesome today."

"Just wait until I get past this pregnancy," she said, "then I'll be really awesome."

"Right," I replied, "but you are always awesome." She kissed me and turned over and closed her eyes.

A Preview of What Is Coming Next

In the next book of the series, Part Three, the warriors will take a field trip to ancient Egypt against their will. They will come face to face with an unknown force that is turning their world upside down. The leaders lives will come crashing down and the team will divide. However, in order to succeed and survive, we all know they have to stand united. Can they put their differences aside to stand united against a force greater than anything the world has ever seen? They are going to make an unbelievable DISCOVERY and they are going to REALIZE that there lives are changed forever.

Mission 7: Ancient Egypt

Mission 8: Discovery

Mission 9: Realization

COMING SOON

Series Summary

When the United States creates a time machine after a close race with the other superpowers, they want to be the first to test it. The United States wants to make sure that they are the first to time travel, at any cost. Their targets become four young adults that will embark on the journey of a lifetime. However, that journey quickly becomes a nightmare.

The four young adults soon battle through time to save those who are innocent. They discover a group that is trying to take over society using the forces of time. The young adults become an agency to regulate time travel known as the Time Warriors. They are worshipped by the world as those who protect time. However, nothing ever goes smoothly.

It soon becomes apparent that there is more to their team than meets the eye. The truth is, their past was hidden from them, and they really don't know who they are. The world soon turns against them and a conspiracy shines through. The team soon realizes that they were setup from day one, and they embark on a quest to figure out who is responsible. The world of the warriors comes crashing down and they are forced to embark on the greatest challenge ever, proving their innocence. The team carries out twelve missions from the experiment to the final battle. In the process, they discover the secret of Atlantis, battle with the armies of the zodiac, visit a prehistoric paradise numerous times, battle with the Master of Time and his followers, take a field trip to ancient Egypt, and battle the four natural elements and the evil Karma. The final battle brings them face to face with Father Time.

Perfection

Written by Tom Tancin

Chapter One

“The company is named G.O.D. and quite appropriately. They are the leaders in the field of genetics, even creating designer babies. Genetics of Design was founded by the two brightest geneticist the world has ever seen. They discovered the way to create the child you dream of, down to the last hair on his or her body. They are able to manipulate any gene on any chromosome. Because of them, every genetic disease ever heard of is on the verge of extinction. However, for as much good as they do, they have that much or more energy for causing problems. They have walked the line of traditional moral values and they are going to cross it now. We have reason to believe they are trying to create 'perfect' organisms. In other words, they are looking to find the best traits for every gene and combine them to create 'perfection'”.

"Can they create perfection," Sherry asked.

"If there is perfection, yes," John replied, "they are the best. But you see, perfection might just be an attempt, there may be no such thing. And if they attempt, the problems will arise. The moral values involved are tremendous. We'll have every religious group in the world jumping down our throats. Not to mention congress, the supreme court, and the president on top of that. And that is just to do with our country."

"So," Sherry said, "what do you expect me to do?"

"I need you to go undercover," John explained, "and try to find out how far this perfection shit is going to go. Supposedly they mentioned it; but that doesn't mean it is going anywhere. The company is rich but it needs support from the world to keep the money it has. They are making money off the diseases they are curing, but if they lose support of the world, any other company will jump in on the opportunity. And trust me, there are plenty of companies looking to do that. The only way this becomes a problem is if they can rally the support from the world. I need you to find out if this is for real and how they plan to get support so we can stop it before it happens."

"Right," Sherry replied. "And how do I pose in a company full of geniuses?"

"They're looking for a lab assistant for a top secret project," John told her. "They are looking for someone who is willing to disappear for a few months. The person they are looking for needs to have a degree in biology, with a severe interest in genetics. Now you have the degree, you just have to pretend to have the interest. Can you handle this?"

"Yeah," Sherry responded, "I can do this."

"Good," John replied, "then gather up what you need. I'll send you the paperwork in a few hours." Sherry got up and walked to the door. She stepped outside the door and closed it behind her. Then she turned to look straight at the door.

"John Steinbeck," she read the sign, "Intelligence Coordinator." Sherry walked to the lobby and poured herself a cup of coffee.

"So how long have you worked for the CIA now," Ryan asked her. Sherry turned to face the man questioning her. Ryan was young, and for her that meant late twenties. He was well toned and attractive with a boyish charm.

"Two years," she told him.

"And this is your first mission," he said with surprise.

"I'm not your typical CIA agent," she explained. "I started out in the Environmental Protection Agency, but then I got transferred here because they wanted a biologist for the CIA to watch G.O.D."

"So what were you doing for the last two years," Ryan questioned.

"Learning the ropes of the CIA," she said as she took a sip of the coffee she had just mixed with milk and sugar. Where were you for the last two years?"

"Undercover," he told her.

"Do you mean undercover or under the covers," she asked.

"Funny," he replied as he chuckled. "I was working on a robbery case."

"Why didn't you ever talk to me before," she wanted to know.

"I don't talk to agents that don't carry out missions," he answered.

"If you don't work, for real that is, then you aren't worth the time. But see, now that you have your first official mission, you are worth the time."

"I'm glad you feel that way Ryan," she replied.

"Besides," he added, "I'm your partner."

"My partner," she laughed, "hah! I work alone."

"Not according to John," Ryan stated. "See according to him, you have the biology background, but you need experience with how to carry out a mission for the CIA. So I am going to cover that aspect."

"And how much do you know about biology," Sherry asked.

"Biology," Ryan replied, "is the study of life. That is all I know. I barely passed it in college."

"Wonderful," Sherry continued, "you'll fit right in." She chuckled as she walked to her office.

"Good morning," the secretary said as Steven and Anna walked into the building.

"Morning," they both replied quickly as they rushed by. They were running late for the meeting and they were crucial. After all, they were the owners of the most advanced genetics company in the world. They studied genetics together for the past thirteen years at some of the most prestigious schools in the world. And for the last eight, they ran the most advanced, yet most controversial, genetics company the world had ever seen.

They quickly made their way to the elevator and chose to go to the sub-floor where the conference rooms were located. The sub-floor was located between the basement and main floor. The elevator door opened and they made their way to the fourth door on the right. Everyone in the room stood up as they entered and made their way to the front of the room. Steven sat down as Anna took her coat off and then sat down. Everyone else followed their lead and took their seats. A young woman hustled over to Steven and Anna and filled the coffee cups in front of them. The room was engaged in random conversation while Steven and Anna prepared themselves for the meeting.

"My wife and I went to a great restaurant last night," Nick told Andrew. Nick was the chairperson of the molecular biology department at G.O.D.. Andrew was the chairperson of the chemistry department.

"Where was it," Andrew asked.

"Just down the road," Nick answered. "It was really fancy and quite expensive, but they have extremely good food."

"We'll have to go sometime," Andrew said. "It will be nice for you and your wife to have dinner with my wife and I."

"It would be nice," Nick agreed. "We don't get out much and it would help us relieve some stress."

"Two strong men like you can't possibly be stressed," Jamie said as she smiled and joined their conversation. Jamie was the chief zoologist at G.O.D. and she was a single woman still searching the market.

"I'm flattered," Nick said as he returned the smile. "But what do you know about stress anyway? I mean, you are just a zoologist."

"Just a zoologist," she responded. "What is that supposed to mean?"

"You can't possibly have as much stress as the chair of molecular biology," Nick continued.

"Or chemistry," Andrew added.

"I'm not going to argue that point," Jamie told them. Steven stood up and searched the room. He checked to make sure everyone was present. At every meeting, each of the chair people were required to be present. In addition to Nick, Andrew, and Jamie, there was Becky, the chief ecologist. Becky made sure to spend as little time at work as possible. She was newly married and didn't want her job to interfere.

Amy was the chair of microbiology. Amy had a rough life, a few broken relationships, and no family to turn to. Amy lived at the company and her job was all she had. Finally, there was Doug, the chair of genetics. He had the most intense and important job in the company. Steven and Anna were always breathing down his neck to make sure he was doing a perfect job. He had been married a few times but his job always got in the way. He has a couple of kids but no time for them. Steven continued his search around the room. He looked for the intern, a young college guy that pretty much did all the errands for the company.

"Where is Jason," Steven asked his secretary as she entered the room and sat down.

"He called in sick this morning," Estelle answered.

"This is the third day in a row if I am not mistaken," Steven replied.

"That's correct sir," Estelle told him.

"Is he seriously ill," Anna asked with concern.

"I don't think so ma'am," Estelle replied. "He didn't sound ill on the phone. I believe he is partying too hard at night."

"Call the university," Steven ordered Estelle and she wrote it down. "Tell them that he has not shown up for three days and we want a replacement intern."

"Yes sir," she said as she stood up and left the room. She closed the door behind her.

"Alright, let's begin," Steven spoke over the group. They all quieted down and waited. "All I want to accomplish this morning is to hear from Doug and Jamie about their experiment with the mouse."

"It was unsuccessful again," Doug reported and waited uncomfortably for Steven's response.

"What is wrong," Anna replied.

"With all due respect Anna," Jamie took over, "we are dealing with a living creature. We can't expect everything to go as planned."

"This is a perfected procedure," Steven raised his voice. He was angry with her questioning of the procedure. "Nothing can go wrong! We worked long and hard on this procedure and it is perfect!"

"We are dealing with a living creature," Jamie replied, "perfection doesn't exist. Nature doesn't allow for perfection. There are mutations which cause imperfection. It is a basic idea."

"But we control nature," Steven told her.

"No," Jamie told him with frustration, "we manipulate it. We are only human. We can't create another living thing to be perfect when we are not perfect ourselves."

"It's a mouse," Steven screamed in anger. "If you can't control a mouse what kind of scientist are you?"

"A human one," Jamie answered. "I am only human. And so is everyone in this room which is why we can't create perfection. There is no such thing; it doesn't exist."

"If it doesn't exist," Steven said with force as he stood up, "then you'll have to invent it." He looked around the room and made sure that everyone knew how angry he was. "You all have two weeks. If, in two weeks, we don't have a perfect mouse in our lab you are all fired! Do you understand me? You will all work together for the next two weeks because if you don't find or create perfection, whichever you prefer, you are all fired!" Steven stormed out of the room and Anna followed.

"That's what I know about stress," Jamie told Nick and Andrew.

Chapter Two

"Hello my name is Estelle and I'm calling from Genetics of Design in regards to an intern you have place at our company," Estelle explained.

"Yes, Jason Smith," the woman on the other line replied. "What about him?"

"He hasn't been showing up for the last few days and Mr. Thomas would like a replacement," Estelle continued. "He hasn't been ill, or at least it doesn't appear that he has. Mr. and Mrs. Thomas take their company very seriously and they will not allow for a college kid to take advantage of them."

"I understand," the lady said. "Maybe I can talk to Jason and have him shape up."

"I'm sorry but Mr. Thomas wants a replacement," Estelle informed her. "He feels that Jason had enough tries to stay at G.O.D.. Obviously he is not dedicated to his field. We request his dismissal from our company and a replacement to fill the vacancy."

"I'll take care of it and get back to you," the lady told her.

"Thank you very much," Estelle replied. Estelle hung up the phone and marked down the date and time she called. She also wrote herself a note that the university would be calling with a replacement.

"Hi," a man's voice said from behind Estelle. Estelle turned around in her chair and looked to see a young man and woman standing before her.

"Can I help you," Estelle greeted them.

"My name is Ryan McAllen," the young man told her, "and I am the person who applied as an intern. I filed the paperwork last week."

"Oh yes," Estelle replied as she grabbed the folder from the front of her desk. "I have it right here. It is even approved by Mr. Thomas. And who are you?" Estelle turned her attention to Sherry.

"I'm applying for the job as a lab assistant here at Genetics of Design," Sherry told her. "I also filed paperwork a few days ago. You called me in today for an interview."

"Sherry Freeman," Estelle said, "yes. I'll see if Mr. Thomas is ready." Estelle picked up the phone and pressed '1' and then put the phone to her ear. She waited for an answer.

"Hello," Steven answered the phone.

"Mr. Thomas, I have a Sherry Freeman here for an interview," Estelle told him.

"Send her in," Steven instructed. Estelle hung up the phone and turned to Sherry.

"You may go in," Estelle told her. "He is in the main office. It is the last office on the right." Estelle pointed down a hallway and Sherry followed the finger with her eyes. "Mr. McAllen you may want to go with her and introduce yourself to Mr. Thomas."

"Thank you very much," Sherry responded as she took in the name inscribed on the plate on the desk. Sherry led Ryan down the hall to the last office on the right.

Sherry took the liberty to knock on the door and waited for a response.

"Come in," Steven responded. Sherry opened the door and entered the large room. There were various secretaries buzzing around the room. Steven sat at a desk across from Anna. Anna turned to face the visitors. "You must be Sherry," Steven continued.

"Yes sir," Sherry replied. "And this is Ryan McAllen." Ryan stepped up to be in line with Sherry.

"Your secretary told me to come and introduce myself to you," Ryan told him. "I am the intern you asked for last week."

"Oh yes," Anna replied, "I forgot to tell you Steven. I found Ryan in a list of applications on Estelle's desk and he looked like the guy we were looking for." Steven picked up the phone and pressed '0'.

"Estelle," Steven said, "call the university back and cancel the intern, we have one." Steven hung up the phone and looked back to Ryan. "Thank you Mr. McAllen," Steven continued, "please wait in the hall."

Ryan left and closed the door behind him. "Have a seat," Steven instructed Sherry. Sherry walked nervously to the chair and sat down.

"Thank you," Sherry said.

"I looked at your file last week and was impressed with your work," Steven explained.

"Thank you," Sherry replied.

"I think you would make a great lab assistant for our next project," Steven told her. "You would have to relocate for a few months. Would that be ok?"

"I would like to have a chance to talk to my husband and son, but I am used to moving for my previous jobs. I don't think it would be a problem at all."

"Let me ask you why you want to work here over the EPA."

"Because I have a passion for genetics and molecular biology. I always did, but the EPA seemed like the right choice at the time. However, when I saw this opportunity, I knew this was for me."

"It will be a pay cut from lead scientist in the water department of the EPA. You do realize that."

"Yes sir. I am willing to start low on the food chain in order to get where I want to be."

"And where is that?"

"I would one day like to be a leading geneticist."

"Well this is certainly the place to start. As far as I am concerned, you are hired." Sherry was ecstatic and smiled with the news. "Unless my wife has anything to ask."

"I think she is perfect for the job," Anna said. Sherry stood up with a smile.

"Thank you both," Sherry said.

"You can meet Estelle," Steven told her, "she'll show you around to some of our employees. That way you get a feel for how the company works." Sherry made her way out to the hall and Ryan stood up from the chair.

"So," Ryan asked with impatience.

"I got the job," Sherry told him.

"That's great," Ryan exclaimed.

Chapter Three

"**O**k darling," Jamie said as she took the mouse from her cage. "Let's make you a perfect baby. And if you cooperate, I'll get to keep my job." She placed the mouse down on the table and injected a needle into her. The mouse squirmed with the pain. "Just a few seconds baby," Jamie said as she closed her eyes in disgust. "I'm sorry, but I have to do this. I promise, you won't feel anything in a few minutes." She waited for the mouse to stop moving and then she grabbed her equipment from the drawer in her desk. She had become so skilled at this procedure, she hardly ever lost a mouse. There was a knock on the lab door. "Come in," Jamie said. The door opened and Estelle entered with a man and a woman behind her.

"Jamie," Estelle began, "this is Ryan and Sherry. Sherry has a biology degree and she is applying for a job. Ryan is applying for an internship while he is studying biology in college. Anna told me to turn them over to you so they can learn the ropes." Jamie knew what that meant. Tell them how they design the mouse offspring but not how they are working on perfection. Steven and Anna had drilled the employees thousands of time on what to say and what not to say. Estelle left and closed the door behind her. Ryan was looking around, taking in the surroundings. It was a pretty large lab, and had some advanced microscopes.

"My name is Jamie," she told them as she put gloves on. "I am the chief zoologist here at GOD. We are currently working on designing a mouse embryo with some of the traits we want. My job, as the zoologist, is to knock the mouse out and extract her eggs. That is what I am preparing to do. I put her to sleep just minutes ago, she'll be out for about an hour."

"The mouse can survive the procedure," Sherry said with astonishment.

"Yes," Jamie replied, "I perfected a procedure that allows the mouse to live. I hardly ever lose a mouse. I couldn't do this if I had to kill them intentionally." Jamie put the mouse under the dissecting scope. She made the incision and picked up a thin tube-like structure. "This takes the eggs out of the mouse and allows me to place them in a test tube." She put the eggs in the test tube and put it in the test tube rack. Then she got the stitches and sewed the mouse up.

"Now what," Ryan asked.

"The next step is to take the eggs up to the genetics lab," Jamie answered. "Up there they'll insert the genes that we are interested in into

the egg. I don't know much about it, but they'll explain it upstairs."
Jamie took the tube with the eggs in it and led Sherry and Ryan out of the
room and down the hall.

"What genes are they interested in," Sherry asked.

"Various genes," Jamie replied. "Sometimes they improve the
speed of the animal, other times they improve one of its senses. For
example, they may increase the mouse's ability to smell so that it has an
easier time finding a piece of cheese when running through a maze." They
got to the elevator and waited for the door to open.

"What is the point of doing this," Ryan questioned with curiosity.
"How does it benefit us if we can have a mouse that can smell a piece of
cheese better?"

"It benefits us," Jamie explained, "because it shows us that we can
do it. We are scientists Ryan, we investigate and invent things. This is
just one more experiment that we were able to succeed at." They got in
the elevator and Jamie pressed the button for the seventh floor.

"But what purpose does it serve," Ryan asked. "I mean other than
for your own satisfaction at succeeding at another experiment."

"If we can do this with a mouse," Jamie continued, "we can do it
with any organism. And think of the possibilities. We already can cure
almost any genetic disease, now we will be able to cure all kinds of
problems that aren't classified as diseases." The door opened and Jamie
led them out of the elevator down the hall.

"But do we have a right to do that," Ryan replied. "Should we be allowed to fix nature's mistakes? Isn't that like playing God?"

"It is viewed like that, yes," Jamie told him. "But you need to look past the fact that we are fixing what nature wanted and look at the fact that we are saving lives. We are enhancing organisms to live happier, more successful lives. What is wrong with that?" Ryan thought for a moment without responding. Jamie opened the door to the genetics lab and they walked in.

Inside there were highly advanced machines everywhere. Ryan tried to take in his surroundings and he held back from asking a thousand questions. A tall man in his early forties, in fact he is forty-three years old walked over to them. "Doug, this is Sherry and Ryan," Jamie told him. "Sherry and Ryan this is Doug. He is the chairperson of our genetics department. He is going to explain the next step. I have to go back down to my lab. I will see you two later." Jamie walked out of the lab and closed the door.

"Now," Doug began, "we are going to design the mouse of our choice." He led them over to a computer sitting in the middle of the lab on a table. He sat down in the chair and pulled the keyboard tray out. He typed in a password and waited for the screen to load.

"This computer holds a database to every gene in all of the organisms that we have mapped," Doug explained. "I can type in any trait I am looking for and the computer will access the database and tell me exactly where to find the gene in the organism's DNA."

"Do you have access to every organism on the planet," Ryan asked.

"We haven't even found every organism on the planet," Sherry quickly answered the question. "You know that Ryan." She looked at him and signaled him to cover up his mistake.

"That's right," Ryan continued. "I forgot that we are still searching for new species everyday. I spoke without thinking."

"We only have a certain number of species in the database," Doug replied. "Our team, and other companies around the world, are adding to the database everyday. However, we are only interested in the model organisms."

"Model organisms are the ones that best suit your research," Sherry responded. "They are the organisms that are easiest to work with, yet they correspond with what you are trying to do."

"Exactly," Doug told her.

"What model organisms are you working with currently," Sherry questioned for curiosity.

"Well mainly mice," Doug replied. "See we have a team working on finding a way to cure genetic diseases, as well as a team to alter viruses and bacteria so they are harmless to humans. We are testing all of that, at least when we can, on mice. Other than that, we are starting to work with primates. But back to what we are working on right now." Doug started typing certain things into the computer but Sherry wasn't sure what it was.

"What are you doing," Ryan asked.

"I am programming in the traits we are interested in for this mouse," Doug answered. "Once I program the traits in, the computer prints out a map of the mouse's genome with the location of the genes for those traits mapped. Then another computer receives the message from this computer and it prints out the sequence of the genes and other DNA sequences that will give us the desired trait. Included are all of the enzymes to cut and paste the segments of the DNA. Basically, with this printout, all our molecular biologists have to do is follow the instructions. With these computers, we are eliminating the trial and error of the experiments." Doug continued to type. "Feel free to look around," Doug told them. "This process will take some time."

Sherry walked away from the computer and started to explore the lab. Ryan followed. "Could you explain that in English," Ryan begged Sherry.

"Basically, he tells the computer what traits he is looking for," Sherry began. "For example, maybe they are looking to enhance the mouse's sense of smell. So what he does is he tells the computer that he is looking for the genes that have to do with the mouse's sense of smell. The computer prints out a map of the mouse's genome."

"What's a genome," Ryan asked.

"The genome is the entire set of chromosomes," Sherry replied. "It is the entire sequence that makes an organism. On that map, the computer highlights areas that are useful in enhancing the mouse's sense of smell. So maybe it is the gene that creates a chemical that creates more nose hairs. I don't know if that is what would actually work, but I am just trying to give you an idea. The computer then sends the message to another computer, which prints out the sequence of the genes and other DNA segments involved. See DNA is made up of genes and spaces that don't code for genes. All of it may be involved, most likely all of it is useful in a certain segment of DNA. If they have the spots highlighted, and the sequences of the bases printed out for them, they can then change what they need."

"I'm still not understanding that last part," Ryan told her.

"Ok," Sherry continued. "Let's say they are looking for the genes to enhance the mouse's sense of smell. Now, the computer finds it on the DNA and marks it for them. The other computer prints out the sequence of bases, the A-C-T-G bases of DNA, and the enzymes needed."

"What's the A-C-T-G bases of DNA," Ryan asked.

"DNA is made up of a sugar, phosphate groups, and nucleotide bases," Sherry replied. "There are four different nucleotide bases. There is adenine, guanine, cytosine, and thymine. Those four bases are what is read and replicated when needed. So, when DNA is read, it is the bases that are read and the sequence of those bases triggers the response. So the second computer gives them that sequence, the one that triggers the response they are looking for based on what they typed into the first computer.

They also get a printout of what to change in order to turn on or turn off the gene they want. So what they can do is use enzymes, which are just complex molecules, to cut segments of DNA. Different enzymes will cut different pieces of DNA and then other enzymes paste segments together. In other words, they can cut and paste the pieces they are interested in, the ones that give the desired traits, together to get the ideal strands of DNA. It's a little more complicated than that, but with the computer's help, they are told what they need and what has to be changed. Their education tells them how to go about changing it. In the past, scientists had to figure out what they needed and what had to be changed on their own by hand and a lot of it was trial and error. You could try to cut and paste hundreds of strands and maybe, if you were lucky, get one that you wanted. Now, with this computer, they can pinpoint and precisely carry out the cutting and pasting. I'm sure there is still some error involved, but not as much as there used to be."

"There is still a lot of error," Doug added as he met them. "We still don't always get what we are looking for."

"But that is just nature working against you," Sherry responded. "You can try all you want, nature is always going to have the final say."

"Not always," Doug replied.

"Yes always," Sherry told him with confidence. "Nature will always have the final say. You cannot prevent mutations and so they are always a factor."

"I agree," Doug said. "Mutations are always a factor, but our molecular biologists are on the brink of stabilizing the replication process of DNA and preventing mutations from taking place."

"Can you do that," Ryan asked.

"We're working on it," Doug told him.

"Nature will always win," Sherry said.

"Well," Doug decided to change the topic of conversation. "I am done programming in the traits I want. Now, the computer is processing it and sending the message to the second computer. In about an hour we will have the printout with everything we need. Then we take the information down to the molecular biologists and they do the dirty work. But for now, you two can go get some lunch in our cafeteria. The cafeteria is on the ground floor. You will have lunch with our ecologist, Becky Watson. After lunch, she will take you to the molecular biology lab and you can see their part of the work."

"Thank you," Sherry said as she walked toward the door. Ryan followed her to the elevator.

"My brain hurts," Ryan complained as Sherry pushed the button to the ground floor and the door closed.

Humans Want It. Nature Won't Allow It.

Perfection

Available May 13, 2006

About the Authors

Tom Tancin was born on January 24, 1984. He lives in Northampton, PA. He is currently a senior at Kutztown University of Pennsylvania studying biology/secondary education. He has a cat, two dogs, a bird, and a hamster. In his free time enjoys writing, listening to music, watching movies, and being with friends and family.

Chris Wolf was born on May 9, 1984. He lives in Danielsville, PA. He currently holds a job. He has a dog and two cats. He is the lead singer for a Christian rock band. He also writes songs for the band. In his free time he enjoys writing songs, listening to music, performing with the band, and spending time with friends.

Destifire Entertainment Projects

Time Warriors: Part One~ ON SALE NOW

Time Warriors: Worshiped~ ON SALE NOW (Special Edition, Internet Exclusive)

Perfection by Tom Tancin~ Available 5/13/2006

Time Warriors: Part Three~ Available 9/9/2006

Time Warriors: Part Four~ Available 12/2/2006

For More Information Visit:

www.destifire.com